AMAZON NUMBER ONE B

ADAM BUSHNELL

It had
new friends
to play with
now.

DOLL

Published in 2019 by
Dark Matters World Publishing

Copyright © 2019 Adam Bushnell

The right of Adam Bushnell to be identified as the author
of this book has been asserted in accordance with the
Copyright, Designs and Patents Act, 1988

All rights reserved. No part of the publication may be reproduced or
transmitted in any form or by any means, electronic or mechanical,
including photocopy, recording, or any information storage and
retrieval system, without permission in writing from the publisher.

This is a work of fiction. Names, characters, places and incidents
either are the products of the author's imagination or are used
fictitiously. Any resemblance to actual persons, living or dead,
businesses, companies, events, or locales is entirely coincidental.

ISBN 978-171242188-8

Cover Design and Interior Layout by designforwriters.com

Chapter One

THE FAMILY SLID ALONG the river in a boat with red, chipped paint. Some flakes fell into the water and looked to the boy like drops of blood. He grinned mischievously. They were finally doing something that *he* wanted to do. They were finally going to La Isla de las Munecas, the Island of Dolls.

"I can't believe you talked us into this, Kyle."

His mother's tone of voice was not angry or firm but rather playful. She was like this on holidays.

"Is a special treat!" the guide laughed, "There are so many fake island now but you go to the real one!"

Fumes belched from the small engine as he turned the rudder slightly. They neared the island.

"Fake islands?" Kyle's mother asked.

His Dad stared on behind dark sunglasses being unusually quiet.

"Si señora," the guide nodded, "Fake islands. Replicas of the original."

"There are loads of them," Kyle interrupted, "Places where tourists will easily part with their money."

"Si, si."

"How do you know all of this?" his mother asked.

"YouTube."

This reply was met by his mother rolling her eyes.

"You say that about everything," she said.

Kyle now rolled his eyes at her.

"So, what was the story again?" she asked, "I know you told us a bit about it last night, but, you know."

"But you had too many tequila cocktails to remember?" Kyle asked.

His mother slapped his arm.

"A man called Julian lived on the island all alone," Kyle said, smiling, "A drowned girl washed up there. She had a doll with her. That was how it started."

"Lo siento, chico," the guide was the one who now interrupted, "That's not quite the story."

Kyle's wasn't angry at being interrupted, if this guide knew the actual real events then all the better. He might even have known the man personally. Kyle smiled again and nodded for the guide to continue. The guide nodded too and went on,

"Don Julian Santana Barrera lived in Mexico City but was a loner. He moved to the Chinampas, the floating gardens between the canals of Xochimico. He wanted to be away from people. The hustle and bustle of the growing city."

"When was this?" Kyle's mother asked.

"In the 1950's señora. Don Barrera was a loner but he travelled by boat to sell his crops that he grew on his island. But one day, on his return from such a journey he found a girl washed up onto the island's beach. Don Barrera alerted the authorities and her body was taken away. The next day, the girl's doll was washed up in exactly the same place. He knew it was hers as it looked just like her. So, Don Barrera decided to put the doll up in a tree as a grave marker for the girl. This was sign of respect."

"But then he became obsessed with the girl's death, right?" Kyle asked.

"Si, si," nodded the guide, "He wished he could have saved her."

"So, he went crazy, right? Started collecting dolls?"

The guide rubbed the stubble on his chin. He was sweating profusely in the afternoon sun. He took a long time to answer but finally said,

"Some think that he did go crazy, they think he started to hear the ghost of the girl on the island. Some think the ghost was in the doll."

The guide made the sign of the cross and kissed the small crucifix that hung on a gold chain around his neck.

Kyle's smile broadened.

"Then he started collecting more dolls and filled the island with them," the boy talked quickly and excitedly, "He put them in the trees and bushes. He decorated his house with them inside and out. He covered the island with dolls."

"Why?" his bewildered mother asked.

"As friends for the ghost of the girl who drowned."

Kyle said this triumphantly. He crossed his hands on the back of his head grinning widely.

"What happened to him?"

The boy leaned forward conspiratorially. In hushed tones he replied,

"He died in the *exact* place the girl had been washed up."

"Is that true?" his mother asked the guide.

"Si señora, in 2001. Floating in the water where the girl was found. No one knows how he died."

"And we are going to the place it all happened!" Kyle declared, "Some people think they can hear the dolls whisper and cry. They've seen their eyes move."

"Trust you to know all of that."

His father had finally spoken. He looked expressionless behind his dark glasses. Kyle saw himself reflected back. Even without sunglasses, the boy usually saw himself in the eyes of his father. It made him feel small. He was always a disappointment in those eyes.

"I wish you'd apply yourself more to some actual work than to this YouTube nonsense."

"Mark," Kyle's mother sighed, "Not now. Not on holiday."

"I thought you'd have grown out of this stuff by now," he went on, regardless, "You're going into Year Nine. There are your options to consider."

His Dad was getting warmed up. The glasses came off and Kyle still looked at himself. Looked at his tiny reflection in those weary eyes.

"You think watching YouTube all day will get you a job? Things are harder than ever now with Brexit. And they're going to get even harder."

"Mark."

The name was spoken harsher this time.

"Don't."

"We've been to museums and art galleries, we've even taken him to see the wrestling and he complained and moaned the whole time."

Mark jabbed his thumb in Kyle's direction.

"This is the most I've heard him speak in two years. When we come to an island filled with bloody dolls!"

Kyle said nothing. The mirror eyes returned their gaze upon him. He just looked back.

"Mark, let's have a nice holiday. It's the first time I've been out of Europe."

"Make the most of it, Denise, it'll be the last time we can afford it."

The glasses were shoved back onto Mark's nose. He sat back using his body to declare he was done as opposed to his voice.

An uncomfortable atmosphere settled onto the boat accompanied by the loud and rhythmic noise from the engine. It chug-chugged happily to itself completely unaware of its tense surroundings.

"We're here," the guide finally said.

It was like the family had briefly forgotten he was there. His voice seemed to startle all three of them. Kyle could not help but smile when the island loomed near. It was surrounded by other smaller islands, each no larger than a roundabout. They circled one of the islands and then approached a larger one.

There was a line of logs that jutted out of the water like patient guards. Above this simple jetty was the family's first sighting of the dolls. Three trees were decorated with about a dozen dolls per tree. There were tied onto the trunk and branches with brown rope. Some dolls wore clothed and others were bleached white by the sun. Their naked plastic flesh was bubbled and burnt.

There were also limbs and decapitated heads of dolls. Eyes were missing and faces were streaked with dirt. Their hair was matted and tattered. They looked like decomposing corpses of children.

"This is so cool!" Kyle exclaimed, "We're here! We're really here!"

The boat slid next to the bank resting on the logs with several small bumps. The engine finally stopped chugging and made several choking sounds. The thick smoke from the engine began to fade drifting up toward the dolls above. The fumes filled the air and made it difficult for the family to breathe.

Mark jumped onto the dried, yellow grass below the doll trees. He grimaced as he looked up at them. He shoved his hands into the pockets of his long shorts and became rooted in his flip flops as the guide helped Denise out of the boat. His dark glasses watched on as the guide offered a hand to Kyle but the boy shook his head and jumped ashore too.

There were beautiful pink flowers bursting from bushes in full bloom. They were at stark contrast to the sight of dolls hanging above. The three trees were twisted and gnarled. They looked to be flinging their limbs in multiple directions as if wanting to throw their macabre decorations into the water, into the air, into the forest, anywhere that was away.

"Is the whole island like this?" Denise asked.

"Si señora," the guide replied while tying the boat to one of the doll trees. "Don Barrera's home is in the middle of the island. I will take you there after you pay."

Mark took off his glasses to let everyone see his eyes roll in their sockets. He reached into one of the pockets of his shorts with one hand and tucked his glasses into his polo shirt with the other. He produced a wallet and asked,

"How much?"

"Three thousand pesos," the guide smiled back, "Good price, señor."

"Three thousand?" Mark spat, "We never agreed to that."

"But we did señor," the guide looked offended, "I tell you that they charge two thousand pesos to take you to the fake island. Then they charge you admission to it like is a museum. Three thousand is boat trip and tour with guide to the *real* island. To Don Barrera's home. Full day trip. Good value, señor. Plus, my boat has an engine. The other boats only have an oar."

"We did agree that price, Mark." Denise said firmly.

"It's only like one hundred and fifty pounds," Kyle said in a small voice, "It's cheaper than that wrestling you made us go to."

"Well why don't you pay for it then?" his Dad shouted in a voice loud enough to send birds flying in fright on the smaller neighbouring islands, "I've paid for this whole holiday!"

Kyle shrugged.

"Fine, I'll pay you back when we're at the hotel. I've got three thousand pesos left."

"From the money *I* gave you!"

Mark took the pesos from his wallet and carefully counted the notes into the guide's hands. He looked visibly annoyed at having to repeat his price to this family.

Denise looked at Kyle and shook her head in an expression of 'leave it'. It was something she and Kyle did frequently to each other.

Kyle took out his phone from his jean shorts and began taking multiple photos. Denise held her camera but did not use it. A first for this holiday.

The guide then walked into the forest of dense trees and the family wordlessly followed. Kyle viewed the entire journey through a screen taking photographs and videos. He stopped for some time at a washing line that stretched between two trees. Many dolls were tied from it, their large baby heads hung slumped forward or to the side making them look like corpses. Baby arms jutted from spiny branches. Baby heads were displayed on twigs like severed heads outside of a medieval castle. The heads and bodies were like a warning to others to follow the rules. The rules of the island. Whatever those might be.

Most of the dolls were plastic but some were fabric with sewn on button eyes. These were severely weather worn and parts were missing, their stuffing oozing out in various places.

Not all the dolls were babies. There were Barbie dolls nailed to tree trunks or hanging from their thick hair.

There were a few porcelain dolls too. They wore old fashioned clothing and had hats on to protect them from the sun. These were slightly more well preserved. Their smooth skin reflected the light making them glow slightly.

"This place is terrifying," Denise said, "I have goosebumps everywhere."

"It's so cool," Kyle grinned back, "I've never seen anything like it. YouTube doesn't do it justice. This place is awesome."

The doll population increased dramatically as they emerged at a clearing with a small, ramshackle hut in the centre. Hundreds of dolls were there. They covered the hut's walls, windows and roof. A wooden decked bridge led from the forest over water and straight to the front door. This bridge was also lined with many dolls but on each fence post only a head was present. The heads were shoved down on each post and were turned to look toward the hut.

"This is the home of Don Barrera."

The guide announced this theatrically and for extra affect he flung out an arm in a gesture indicating that they should go on.

Kyle went first. A smile now tattooed on his face but still using the phone to record every detail of the trip. Mark followed and Denise scuttled behind him. The guide's good humour had returned now and his smile was back.

"Let us go into the home of Don Julian Santana Barrera!"

Chapter Two

THE WALLS OF THE shack were of wooden slats which Kyle thought were similar to his garden fence back home. But here each one bore nailed dolls of every kind. The nails were hammered through thick hair of Barbies or through tough plastic necks and arms. The clothes of other dolls suspended them limply from the slats.

"This is so cool," Kyle grinned, "Check it out."

The boy picked up a doll and held it like some sort of trophy. The guide shook his head.

"These are not to be touched," he said waving a finger from side to side, "They are charmed. They are very blessed."

Kyle placed the doll back where it had come from with something like reverence. There was a shrine like element to the entire island and this hut was the epicentre.

The guide made another grand gesture with his arm for them to go inside. Denise flattened her dress with swift movements of the palm of her hand. The thin material rustled. Mark took off his sunglasses and pushed them down into the front of his polo shirt and smoothed down his thinning hair. Kyle noticed that this was exactly the kind of thing they did before they went into Mexico's Cathedral earlier in the trip.

This made the boy think that the entire island had a sort of religious feel to it. It didn't feel evil, which is what he had been expecting, but rather it was spiritual.

His parents made no move to go inside, other than their bodily suggestions of movement, so Kyle ducked under the low doorway and stepped into the gloom.

There was a broken down chair in the musty single room but the main items were, unsurprisingly, dolls. Tiny dolls were scattered here and there and much larger ones too. Their lifeless eyes coolly observed the arrival of the family and their guide.

Kyle remembered a line from the film Jaws, where the shark hunter compared shark's eyes as 'doll's eyes'. That was exactly right. The eyes of these dolls in the darkness were shark eyes. There was something about them that made him think of silent predators hunting in their black liquid dark surroundings.

On the floor were scraps of newspapers and straw. Barrera must have slept on the floor with the dolls, there was no bed.

The walls and roof were utterly covered in black eyed dolls. The four of them were squashed inside and all looked around the small room with differing expressions. Kyle was wide eyed and grinning. The guide lowered his eyes and held his hands as if standing as some gravestone offering respect. Denise had a furrowed brow and was shaking her head slightly. Mark looked slightly annoyed by the whole thing. But this was a familiar fitting.

The dolls on the floor were heaped on top of one another in little piles but in the centre of the room, sitting on a blanket on a pile of straw, was one single doll. It looked to Kyle like a Nativity scene.

There was a woven bowl sitting in front of the doll. In it was money. Coins and notes. It was an offertory.

"This is Agustinata," the guide nodded toward the doll.

"No way," Kyle gasped, "The first doll?"

The guide nodded his head again a few times.

"The one that belonged to the drowned girl?" asked Denise.

The guide continued to nod.

"I've had enough of this."

Mark pushed past them all and went outside.

"It's ridiculous," he muttered outside, "All this way across the world to come here. All this money."

Everyone ignored him then Denise wordlessly left the shack and joined her husband outside. The guide remained with Kyle. The boy looked at him.

Why was he watching him? Did the guide think he was going to do something? Steal the money perhaps? Take something else?

Kyle's smile faded and returned. He would take something. But not money. The thought hadn't occurred to him before. There was no gift shop at this place but he wanted a souvenir. A doll. He would take it home and show his cousin. She would understand. She loved creepy things as much as him. What had his uncle called him? Not a goth. But he did love gothic things. He had said that he and Emily were *macabre*. Like the piece of music his music teacher had banged on about. Danse Macabre. Wasn't there book called that too?

The guide was staring at him now. Kyle had on a backpack. It was loosely hanging down against his backside. There wasn't much inside. He had a bottle of water, sun cream, a book and a few snacks. Plenty of room for a doll.

Emily would go crazy for it.

Any doll would do. Which was the creepiest? His eyes scanned the room. He was absolutely spoilt for choice. One of them had an eye hanging from its socket. That one. But then another had one eye open and one closed with a huge mane of grey hair around it. It's child face and old woman hair were at stark contrast to one another. There was one with small holes in its naked chest like a speaker. It must have a cord on its back so that it could make a noise like 'mama'. That would be pretty scary too. There was a doll whose face was utterly covered in cobwebs.

The guide coughed. A gesture for Kyle to get going. He had to be quick but how would he do it?

He looked again at the doll covered in cobwebs. Beneath the tiny tangled strands two large and black eyes peered up at the boy. It had matted brown hair and wore a lacey dress complete with a pearl necklace. The doll had a haunted, sad expression. The cobwebs made a veil over her face. That was the one.

Kyle smiled at the guide and turned to leave. He lifted his hand in an 'after you' gesture. Then took out his phone to take more photos. The guide nodded briskly and moved toward the doorway. Kyle dropped his backpack silently onto the straw strewn floor and followed him outside.

His parents were wordlessly standing back to back looking around at the doll decorated trees and bushes. They turned as one to watch Kyle approach.

"Are we done here now?" his Dad barked.

Kyle nodded and smiled.

"Just a few more photos," he said, "You want to be in them?"

"Certainly not." Mark replied.

Kyle laughed and took a few more pictures.

"Where's your backpack?" his mother asked as they began to leave.

"Oh," Kyle said raising his hand to his mouth, "I left it in there."

Before anything could be said he turned and ran back into the shack. He scooped up a doll and shoved it in his bag as the guide appeared behind him.

"Got it," he gasped and turned to push past the guide.

Kyle shouldered the backpack and asked,

"So how long have you been bringing people here?"

"Since 2001," the guide answered, "Since Don Barrera passed away."

"Have you got children yourself?"

"Si, two girls."

"How old are they?"

"Sixteen and eighteen."

"Do they live with you?"

All the while Kyle asked relentless questions the boy walked on the guide followed. Ask people about themselves. That was the advice his cousin Emily had given him. People love to talk about themselves, she had said. If you don't know what to say or if you want to distract someone from something you've done then ask them about themselves. She was amazing at it. She did it in school all the time. He now mimicked her and it was working.

He and the guide led on with his parents following behind. They walked over the bridge, through the forest and toward the tethered boat. The dolls looked on from the trees. They observed one of their own being kidnapped but could do nothing about it.

It made Kyle smile. It was the smile of a reptile. The kind of smile that only emerges when one has done something that one should not. A smile of mischief. A smile of a shark. Or a doll.

The boat bobbed against the wooden posts in the shadow of the doll decorated trees. Meanwhile, Kyle's questions continued. He was determined to distract the guide. He had to get the doll off the island.

"So, what does Xochimilco mean?"

"Is where the flowers grow." The guide relied.

"Like the Frankie Valli song?" Mark asked, perking up slightly.

"I don't know that, senor."

The guide offered his hand and Denise took it, stepping uncertainly into the narrow gondola like boat.

"I take you to the embarcaderos then you can get taxi to your hotel."

"Thank you, erm, what was your name?" Kyle asked.

"Pedro, chico."

"The flowers on the island are beautiful," Denise said.

The dolls looked on with their missing limbs and shark eyes. Kyle looked up at them but then quickly looked away as if guilt was only felt under their lifeless gaze.

"Are the islands all a similar size?"

Kyle resumed his questions. They were not only a distraction for the guide but served to distract himself as well. An ominous feeling of dread was welling inside of him. It was like the one and only time he had stolen money from his father's wallet. He hadn't taken much and hadn't taken it all. There had been seventy pounds in there. The boy could picture the scene clearly.

His Dad's jacket was hanging on the banister of the stairs. His wallet was inside a pocket. His parents were watching television. Kyle had taken the wallet and saw a twenty-pound note, four tens and two fives. He took three of the ten-pound notes and slunk off to his room. He didn't want the money for anything in particular. It wasn't like thirty pounds was something he had planned to take. It was just if he had taken all of it then his Dad would have noticed. He didn't steal it for any other reason than the rush of doing so.

But he hadn't coped well with the guilt. He had spent the money on buying things for his friends. He paid for he and two friends to go to the cinema and bought them treats. He sat through the film feeling terribly guilty.

He hadn't stolen anything since. Until now.

The engine chugged into life and he put the backpack behind the calves of his legs. The bag felt heavy and conspicuous. The boat snaked its way from the tiny island toward even smaller island beyond. It slid over the canals and away from the guilty glare of the suspended little people. It was going to be a long hour-long trip back to the city.

"What the name of the place we're going back to?" Kyle asked to continue to distract himself.

"Mexico City," his Dad snapped back.

His sunglasses were back on but Kyle could feel the roll of his father's eyes behind the black glass.

"Trajinera Pier, chico." the guide replied.

"Ah right, what does that mean?"

"Trajinera is the type of boat. Is a boat that transports goods to and from places. Now is to transport people."

The red painted boat was lined with little yellow chairs. There were ten of them in total. But this boat had been different to all of the others as it was the only one with an engine. Kyle looked at the guide, his parents and then the islands either side of the boat. They were bursting with trees and those same pink flowers from the island with the dolls. The fragrant scent in the air mingled with the fumes from the engine of the boat. The guide wordlessly steered the boat over the brown, calm water.

Kyle pondered his prize. He hadn't taken the cobweb strewn doll after all. The doll he had taken was Agustinata. Icy spiders created goosebumps all over his flesh. What had he done?

Chapter Three

Kyle slipped the backpack on as soon as they neared the pier. Other red and yellow boats lined the port. He wanted to get off the boat as soon as possible. He stumbled and tripped as he stepped onto the concrete pier. It was patterned in spiral shapes and he wanted to run over them to the taxi rank as soon as possible but he had to maintain his cool. For the doll to be discovered now would be disastrous. The boy turned and watched the guide help his mother off the boat and shake his father's hand who was already on the pier next to them.

"Thank you, Pedro," Kyle said extending his hand toward the guide, "That was amazing."

Pedro smiled. His eyes were warm and genuine. They looked into the boy's eyes but then drifted to his backpack. Kyle had to think quickly.

"Can I get a photo with you in it?" the boy asked.

The guide's eyes flicked back to Kyle's face and he laughed.

"No, no, no."

"Please, Pedro," laughed Kyle, "I don't want to forget you. You've been an amazing guide."

The boy slid shoulder to shoulder next to the guide and held up his phone. Pedro looked awkward and wore a strained smile. Kyle took the photo and shook his hand again.

DOLL | 21

"Yes, yes, thanks and all that," his Dad interrupted, "Let's go."

Then they were off. Pedro waved from the pier as the three walked toward the taxi rank. The backpack felt lighter than before and Kyle managed a stupid smile. He had done it. He had the doll. Emily would be thrilled. He would get more YouTube subscribers than ever. He would set up an Agustinata channel. The Mexican doll would be a sensation. The smile broadened. He would be famous. Everyone in school would be so jealous. He had done it.

His parents decided to have a drink in the hotel bar. Kyle told them he was going up to the room to look at the photos from the day. His father mumbled something and his mother nodded and chose a seat.

The elevator journey seemed long. He wanted to look at the doll right away but Kyle felt that this was something needed to be done in the secrecy of the hotel room. At last he arrived and used the card three times to get into the room. Where his hands shaking? They probably where. The adrenaline from what he had just done was racing through his body. His eyes were wide and his heart was pounding. The door closed with a dull clicking sound.

Kyle sat on his parent's large king size bed with the backpack on his lap. His bed was the folded-up sofa. It had been an uncomfortable week. But it now felt worth it. Worth his Dad snoring. Worth the silences and the tension in this room. He then slowly, perhaps reverently, unzipped the black canvas. The white face glowed from within. The boy lifted the doll with great care. He placed it onto the white sheets of the bed and stood up.

Agustinata had completely white skin made from porcelain with raven black long hair. She wore a long midnight black dress with white frills around the collar and sleeves. Her feet were hidden by the folds of the dress but her delicate white fingers poked from the frilly sleeves. She had bright blue eyes framed with black eyeliner and black thin eyebrows. Red lips were pursed into a slight smile and ruddy, red cheeks sat either side. Her fixed gaze was impassive. Kyle thought that she did look slightly sad though.

Was this an exact copy of the drowned girl? Did she look exactly like this? Did she wear the same long black dress? It occurred to Kyle that the doll wore the clothes of someone in mourning.

He picked her up and looked at her from different angles. The rest of the dolls on the island were filthy and in various states of decay but Agustinata was not. She was clean and cobweb free. She appeared to be cared for.

Would she be missed? It didn't matter. Even if the guide returned to the island tomorrow and noticed she was gone, so would he. Kyle and his family flew back to England the next day. He had done it.

He returned the doll to his backpack and pulled out his phone. He flicked through the photos from the day but soon got Agustinata out from the bag again. Her hair shimmered. It was thick and recently combed. There were no tangles or knots. Who had been caring for her? The same people that had made donations perhaps. The now familiar stab of guilt was back.

He put her back in the bag and decided to pack. They were leaving early and this would save him being nagged by his parents. They were probably arguing by now and would be back into the room to sit in cold silence for a while. As if summoned by the thought, his mother arrived in the room looking upset. She looked at Kyle but said nothing and began to busy herself in the bathroom behind a locked door.

His father arrived soon afterwards wearing a well-worn look of anger. Kyle ignored him and carried on packing his suitcase.

"You got the money for that stupid trip then?" his father spat at him.

Kyle looked at him and nodded. He pulled his wallet from his bedside table and took out the cash he had. He held this out and Mark snatched it from the boy's hand. He counted it.

"Two thousand, eight hundred."

Kyle shrugged.

"It'll have to do I suppose."

Kyle shrugged again.

His father tutted and got his own case ready to pack. Kyle resumed his own packing and when his father had his back turned the boy slid Agustinata between his dirty T shirts and shorts inside his case.

When his mother finally left the bathroom the three went for an awkward dinner in the buffet restaurant. Kyle went back to the room and watched videos with headphones on. His parents said little to each other.

The next morning, they took a taxi to the airport and then sat on a plane to San Francisco watching their own individual screens with headphones on and saying very little to each other. They continued to do this all the way to Amsterdam and then finally a flight to Newcastle.

Fifteen hours of flight time was passed in silence and that was the way Kyle liked it. Agustinata was Kyle's main thought the whole time. How he would use her to post videos, what he would say. He would be the narrator but she would be the star. He would begin with photos and videos of his trip to the island but then he would go on to tell the story of Don Barrera. After that, Kyle would make up new tales about the doll. Tell stories of what she had done the night before. She would be the new Chucky or Annabelle of YouTube. She might even get noticed enough for a film franchise. It was possible. These things happened. He would show his parents, his teachers, his friends, everyone at school would be so jealous. He would have loads of money.

They got into the car parked for a fortune and began the drive back to home. It wasn't going to be a long journey, forty-five minutes maybe. All three were tired though.

"I've got to stop for fuel."

Kyle's Dad announced this then took a slip road to a service station. He filled up with petrol then inflated the tyres. This seemed like a pointless and time-wasting thing to do when they were all so exhausted and wanted to get home. Kyle was going to say this to his mother but then didn't. In the end, it was his mother who broke the silence.

"Did you enjoy the trip?" she asked wearily.

"Yeah," he replied not looking up from his phone.

"What was the best bit?"

"Guess," he grinned.

"Did your Dad make you pay for it?"

Kyle hesitated a moment or two before answering.

"It doesn't matter," was the reply he finally settled on.

Denise rolled her eyes. Her lips became a thin line. Her brow furrowed. Mark was walking back toward the car examining the receipt. He was utterly absorbed and was nearly hit by a car exiting the garage but he didn't seem to notice. Kyle put in his headphones and turned the volume up as far as it would go. He knew what was coming next. His parents were arguing the moment Mark got into the car. He couldn't hear the exact words and he didn't watch the bodily gestures but he could feel the argument. It was a tense and horrid thing. Kyle was focused entirely upon his phone. Odd words cut through when there were pauses in the video he was watching. Money, Kyle, ungrateful, waste, future, career, money, Kyle, money. The boy shook his head.

He looked up and saw that they were driving too fast.

"Dad," he said.

His voice was small and weak.

His father was pointing an accusatory finger at his mother. One hand on the wheel, the other wildly pointing and shouting. His mother was shouting back. It was so odd to see these two adults sitting in chairs, travelling very fast, while shouting at one another. It seemed absurdly unreal.

The car raced round a bend and the over inflated tyre nudged the kerb. There was a loud bang and the car flew into the air. Kyle dropped his phone and grabbed the back of his head to protect himself. This was not something he had decided to do. It was not something that he had practised or been told to do in lessons at school. It was an instinctive action that had come from somewhere deep inside his mind. A basic human instinct for self-preservation.

The car slammed into the road and span up into the air again. And again. And again.

It rolled onto its roof and wobbled uncertainly on the other side of the road.

The three were suspended by their seatbelts.

Kyle pulled his headphones that hung from his ears.

"Is everyone ok?" his father asked.

His mother made a whimpering noise.

"Can you get your seatbelt off, Kyle?"

He looked at the red release button.

"Yeah, I – I think so," he heard himself say.

Every window was shattered. Beads of glass where everywhere.

"Denise," his father said firmly, "Denise."

"Y – Yes?"

"Are you injured? Are you bleeding?"

"No, no, I'm ok."

"Kyle, are you?"

The boy looked at his hanging body. His mind was racing. Adrenaline coursed through his veins much more intensely now than when he had stolen the doll. The doll. His suspended body looked like those hanging dolls on the island.

"No, I don't think so," he replied.

"We need to get out of this car," his father said in an almost calm voice, "Can you do that?"

It wasn't clear if he was talking to Kyle, Denise or himself. It seemed like a general instruction to them all.

"We need to go now."

Kyle began to fiddle with the seatbelt. He pressed the button and he landed on the roof of the car with a dull thud. The fabric was covered in beads of glass and some of them went into his knees. He didn't feel any pain though so he started to crawl through the back window. He turned to see his mother helping his father to release his seatbelt. Perhaps he could help once he had got out of the car. He heard a thud.

"You've done it," his father gasped, "I'll do yours."

Kyle squeezed himself out of the window. He saw that the car had landed on the wrong side of the road. It was upside down and facing the wrong way. He was almost fully out of the car when he also saw a truck coming toward him. It was the last thing he saw. The brakes screeched and smoke belched from the tyres. The truck slammed into the car and killed all three of them instantly upon impact.

Chapter Four

Emily walked into Flannels and headed straight to the clearance section. She was meeting her friends in an hour. She found the Tommy Hilfiger vest top she wanted and checked the size. A smile found its way upon her face and she went to pay.

She asked for a larger bag than the one offered and a grumpy sales assistant begrudgingly obliged.

Emily was fourteen and on her summer holidays from school. She had taken her options and was going into Year Ten after the summer holidays. She was teased about her hair and she pretended to hate it but really, she liked its auburn colour. Her hair was thick, long and naturally curly but she used her straighteners like a pro every morning. She danced every day and had done since she was five. This made her posture excellent and she carried herself with a raised chin and straight back. To some this appeared to give off a sense of arrogance but this was far from the truth. She was humble and quick to laugh. This made her popular but she was choosy with her friends. The more popular girls at school wanted to be her friend but she couldn't be bothered with the drama of it all. Her Snapchat streak with close friends was high but she didn't try and keep up with every one of her followers.

She posted occasionally on Instagram but usually she just looked at other people's posts. She sometimes took screenshots and posted them to her friends in order to privately, rather than publicly, express what she really thought.

Emily looked over her shoulder. It was ten in the morning and the shopping centre was quiet. There was no one of her age around. She checked both directions then once satisfied there was no one she knew, went inside Primark. She chose leggings and a few tops then quickly paid. She wrapped the brown paper bag up tightly and put it inside the Flannels bag underneath the Tommy Hilfiger vest.

Then she made her way to JD to browse the trainers while she waited for her friends.

She took photos of some that she liked so that she could find them cheaper online later. This shopping trip was not something she did often, much to the frustration of her friends. Much to her own frustration too. But her dance commitments were six times a week. She needed to dance. It wasn't just the physical activity, it was something else. It certainly kept her fit and lean. She ate what she wanted and still had perfectly toned muscles with a slender frame. Her clothes were fitted but not too revealing like some of her friends. It was more that she found the physical movement expressed her emotions better than she could orally. Also, she didn't want to be intense. Some people at school were so intense. They told you *everything*. They analysed *everything*. They asked you nothing but told you every paranoid thought in their head.

Sure, she had her own paranoid moments and experiences with utter bitches, both boys and girls, but dance allowed her to rid herself of any intense emotions. She simply danced it off. It made her feel better in every way both physically and mentally.

The Nike Air Max 97 juniors were tempting. They looked chunky and yet neat at the same time. The Adidas Gazelles were smaller and classic. She took some photos then slid her iPhone into her back pocket of her jeans and moved on.

She wasn't rich but she saved her money and spent it occasionally on days like this. She had bought what she had wanted and was happy to spend the rest of the day helping her two friends, Ngozi and Meg, choose what they wanted. As this was such a rare treat, Emily had wanted to make sure she bought the Tommy Hilfiger top before anything else. She liked designer clothes. Not because she wanted to fit in, that was part of it she had to admit it just to herself, despite her best efforts to pretend otherwise, but rather because they fit better, looked better and lasted longer. The Primark stuff she got were to accessorize cheaply but these clothes were simply not the same. Although, the New Look vest top under her Pink hoodie had cost two pounds and had survived six washes now.

A sales assistant was following her. She hated that but refused to be intimidated. She smiled at her and said hello. The girl sneered back and slinked off. She had thickly drawn eyebrows and far too much fake tan. The orange glow of her seemed to remain even after she left. The smell too.

Emily laughed inwardly. Fake tan was not something she needed to worry about with her skin. That was another advantage of her colouring. She did use foundation but only the expensive stuff and sparingly. She hated her freckles and tried to cover them up, mostly unsuccessfully, but would rather have them than be plastered in product. The sales assistant had obviously used cheap fake tan and the smell of digestive biscuits was thick in the air.

Emily turned and left the shop. She set off to meet her friends. They were getting the bus but she had been given a lift earlier by her step Dad, Paul. He wasn't really her step Dad, as he and her Mum weren't married. To her friends she described him as her 'friend' but he really was like her Dad. He gave her lifts and money but it was his time he gave her most of.

Most of her friends had the same set up. It was something they talked about a lot and this helped her know it was all just normal.

Ngozi and Meg were sat in huge massage chairs outside of North Face. They were laughing and looked tiny in the oversized black leather chairs. They waved as they saw Emily approach. She waved back and smiled warmly.

"What time you get here?" Meg asked.

"A little while ago," Emily replied, "Paul dropped me off too early so I bought this."

She held up the Tommy Hilfiger vest top as Meg and Ngozi stood up to have a look. It was a dark blue with white straps bearing the Hilfiger logo several times down each strap.

"Was that in the sale?" asked Ngozi.

"Yeah from eighty to forty," smiled Emily and raised her eyebrows several times.

"I'm gonna see if they have it in red," Ngozi said nodding.

"Let's start there then," Meg laughed and pushed the other two girls.

As they walked, the shopping centre began to get busy. Groups of teenagers, families with push chairs and an incredible number of mobility scooters soon filled the aisles.

"Did you see Happy Death Day?" Meg asked.

Ngozi replied with a question,

"Is it on Netflix?"

"Nah, Sky Box Office," grinned Meg mischievously.

"You are literally the only person I know that still has Sky," Ngozi said shaking her head, "How can your parents afford that?"

"My Dad has the football," Meg laughed, "And BT Sport. It costs loads."

"I've seen it," Emily butted in, "It was alright."

"How've you seen it?" Meg asked.

"Kodi box," she smiled, "And Annabelle Creation too."

"What was that like?"

Emily looked at Meg and shrugged her shoulders.

"OK. Can't wait to see Hereditary. That looks good."

"There's The First Purge too," added Ngozi, "Might be ok."

"The first Purge film was good but the others haven't been all that," Emily said, "There's an Amazon TV series too. Dunno what that'll be like. The new Halloween might be ok though. Back to John Carpenter's original characters, you know."

"The Rob Zombie ones were good though," Meg said, "Savage."

The girls laughed and went into the shop.

"You seen the new Suspiria advert?" Ngozi asked. "Looks weird."

"Looks amazing you mean," Emily stopped walking, "Amazing."

The other girls stopped too.

"You seen the original?" she asked them.

They shook their heads.

"I'll loan you the DVD."

"Who watches DVDs anymore?" asked Meg.

"It's the only way to get most of the classics. I love old school."

"When was it made?" laughed Meg, "In like the eighties?"

"Seventies. 1977. Such a good film though."

Emily was nodding seriously.

"The new film looks like it's going to be good. The advert looks a lot like the Italian original even though its Hollywood. The director seems to be keeping the same style. Not the same crazy bright colours though."

"You're such a geek," Ngozi laughed.

"It's the same director as that Call Me By Your Name film," Emily added.

"Not helping," Ngozi went on, "That was a good film though. Where's the sales stuff?"

Emily walked over and the girls followed. The rest of the day was spent shopping, buying iced tea from Starbucks and eating at Yo Sushi. She bought nothing else but did help her friends choose outfits, giving honest opinions and advice for accessories. Then, at 3pm, Emily's phone, which almost constantly lit up with notifications, mainly from Snapchat, was called five times.

"Why is Paul calling me so much?" she said in exasperated tones, "He's such a *Dad*."

She shoved the phone back into her back pocket and went on. Her phone was called a further five times but the vibrate was off and she didn't notice until she checked her streak a few minutes later.

"He's kept calling," she said, now a little worried, "I'd better call him back."

She lifted the phone to her ear.

"What?" she said when he answered on the first ring.

Her furrowed brow fell. All colour drained from her face. She had only heard one word and that was 'accident'.

"Is it Mum?"

She was frozen for a moment.

"Ok, then who? What accident? Never mind 'you'll tell me at home'. Tell me now."

Her hand went to her mouth. Ngozi and Meg stood like statues.

"How?"

She ended the call in less than a minute but the seconds had dragged on like weeks for the two friends.

"What's happened?" Ngozi asked in a small voice.

Meg put her hand on Emily's shoulder.

"Kyle's been in an accident," Emily whispered.

"Is he ok?" asked Ngozi.

"I don't know. Paul's on his way here now. I've got to go."

"We'll come with you."

Meg nodded in agreement. The three walked hurriedly toward the multi storey car park on the ground floor. They rushed through T K Maxx and saw Paul's car idling in a disabled bay.

"Which hospital is he in?" Emily asked as soon as the door was open.

"Durham," Paul replied, "I'll take you home first. Your Mum is waiting for us. Girls, can I drop you back before?"

"It's ok," said Ngozi, "We'll walk from yours."

Meg nodded.

The three were sat in the back. Meg and Ngozi were either side of Emily holding her hands. She was lost in thought. Being friends with your younger, male cousin wasn't cool but she and Kyle were close. She felt like she had been with him on his Mexican holiday. His funny posts always made her laugh. His trip to that island of dolls looked amazing. He had messaged her to say he had brought something back that she would love too.

They exited the car park and drove quickly down the motorway. Paul usually drove slower than her Mum, especially when there were passengers, yet he was driving fast. The girls didn't speak all the way back. There was no music on and everyone was lost in their own thoughts.

Paul pulled up onto the drive. Meg and Ngozi hugged Emily as they left and she followed Paul into the house. Her Mum was standing in the living room. Tears where in her eyes and her hands were clasped over her mouth. It looked like she was holding the words in. Emily knew at once that Kyle was dead.

Chapter Five

Emily rushed over and put her arms around her Mum. Paul stood awkwardly to one side for a time.

"Catherine," Paul eventually said quietly.

He came over and put his hands onto Emily's Mum's back. Then he hugged them both.

They stood like this for several minutes. Emily and her Mum openly crying with Paul holding every shaking sob. Then it was Emily who broke back first.

"How?" she asked through tear streaked eyes, "What happened?"

Paul guided them both to the sofa. Catherine didn't speak and had her eyes closed the whole time. Paul described what the police had told them. He had listened to the call when Catherine had put it on speaker for him to hear. They had crashed, a truck had collided with them and they died instantly at the scene. The ambulance had transported them to the mortuary at the hospital where a doctor pronounced them officially dead. That was it.

He put this as best he could but the facts were what they were. Catherine was close to her sister Denise. There was only two years age difference, Denise being the younger sister. They had lived barely three streets away from each other since leaving home and even went to the same university. They were so different from one another yet extremely close. It was incomprehensible that this could have happened. Kyle was round at the house several times in a week to do homework, watch a film, hang out with Emily or just to say hi. He and Emily didn't speak much at school but at home it was entirely different.

Now he was gone. All three of them were gone.

An hour passed without words. Then Emily decided that she didn't want to be with her Mum or Paul. She wanted to be alone. None of it made sense and she needed to process it. She needed to be in her room with the lights off. She felt that she wanted to be a shadow in the dark.

She let go of her Mum and stood up. Catherine looked at her daughter through watery eyes.

"I'm going to my room," Emily said.

"Em," Catherine squeaked and held up her hands. "Em."

Em. Her Mum hadn't called her that in years.

"Sorry Mum."

Emily almost ran from the room. She heard Paul say, 'leave her'. She threw herself onto her bed and pushed her face into her pillow. Nothing made sense. Her world felt like the 'other world' in Stranger Things. She felt as if she was in the Upside Down. She was no longer in the real world but rather in some place unknown to her. A place where everything was the same but different. A place where even the air tasted unreal. A place without Kyle.

Her face remained smothered by her pillow for some time. Eventually Emily turned onto her back. She looked around her room. Her perfume, her makeup, her clothes, her straighteners, her mirrors, her leotards, her medals . . . her stuff; it was all so meaningless.

Paul appeared at the door. He did this weird knock he always did where he drummed his fingers a few times on the wood rather than actually knocking. She supposed it was to let her know it was him. He pushed the door opened a little and peered in.

"Can I get you anything?" he asked softly.

"No," she replied quietly.

He pushed the door closed but not fully closed and thudded downstairs. She should go and check on Mum but she just couldn't at that moment. The remainder of the day was a myriad of lost thoughts. A conundrum she couldn't possibly ever solve. It was the beginning of grief. She had heard of five stages that people were meant to go through. First was denial but this was undeniably real. How could this not be real? It was too painful to be denied. Then there was meant to be anger and bargaining and depression and acceptance. She didn't know who she could bargain with. God perhaps? But what was she hoping for? A resurrection?

She settled on anger and depression. They were a better fit for her right now. She would merge these two stages; stage two and four as one. She would wear only these two for now.

Darkness finally found its way into the sky. Its black ink spread wide over the view from her bed. It was comforting and was the first thing that felt right. Despite her best efforts sleep enveloped her.

She woke in the night and remembered it all. She adjusted her eyes and looked around her room. A duvet was pulled over her and the curtains had been closed. In the gloom of her room she could hear faint crying from the room next door. She got up and physically shook her head as if trying to rid the spiders of her mind. But everything came creeping back.

"Mum," she whispered at the door.

"Emily," Paul said and was at the door in seconds, "You ok? Can I get you anything?"

She shook her head and pushed past him. Her Mum sat up and held out her arms. The pair hugged and Paul stood nearby.

The funeral was two days later, which seemed whirlwind fast to

Emily. All three bodies were cremated. Catherine read a eulogy and managed it without crying. At the end of the service she broke down and was held by Paul and Emily. It had been decided that they would scatter all three sets of ashes at the beach sometime soon. The ashes were inside three ceramic urns. These were placed upon a table in the living room for one night.

Emily found them sinister and disturbing things. For someone who had always been fascinated by creepy things the reality of death was not something she wanted to ponder upon. Horror films and ghost stories were something entirely different. They were meant to entertain and scare you a little. They made you jump and aroused a morbid curiosity but actual death was just so final and clinical. It was all just so . . . sad.

Her grandparents had fussed over her, family friends had too. Ngozi, Meg and other friends had been in constant touch. But Emily was just so sick of it. She didn't want to keep up her streaks on Snapchat. She had no idea what she would say. The thoughts of taking photos of herself were unimaginable. She didn't want to look at anyone's posts on Instagram. She just wasn't interested.

Eventually she decided to delete her accounts. But then she didn't. She wanted to take a look at Kyle's posts. Not now. But later. They would still be on there. To delete herself from having access to them was to rob of herself of something precious. To rob herself of part of his memory. She sat on her bed, lost in thoughts when Catherine came up to her room.

"Emily?"

"Yeah, come in."

"I've got a bag with some of Kyle's things."

A Tesco bag with pictures of herbs on it was in her Mum's hand.

"Oh," was all she could manage.

"It's things Paul and I sorted. He's going to deal with the rest of the house next week. Maybe the week after."

"Oh."

"I'll put it over here."

She put the bag next to a set of drawers. Emily could see some books, DVDs and a few other things like Pop Vinyls poking out. She let out a long sigh.

"Just look at them when you're ready," Catherine said as she sat on the bed, "Can I get you anything?"

"You sound like Paul."

Catherine smiled slightly.

"We're going to scatter the ashes tomorrow."

Emily nodded.

"Invite who you like."

She nodded again.

"Hungry?"

She shook her head.

Catherine hugged her daughter. They stayed like this for a while.

"I'll bring you a hot chocolate."

Emily nodded and rolled over, hugging herself. Catherine went off and Emily turned to look at the bag with Kyle's things in it. The bag loomed largely in her room. She heaved herself off the bed and put a hoodie over the top of it. Then she went downstairs to join her Mum. Maybe she would watch TV with her for a while. She hadn't done that in years. The only thing she had watched with her Mum recently was The Greatest Showman at the cinema. But as for TV? She just could not remember the last thing they had watched. High School Musical maybe. The thought of it made her smile.

The microwave beeped annoyingly. Emily took the hot chocolate before her Mum could and said,

"Let's watch a film."

Catherine's surprise was apparent.

"Did I just hear that right?" Paul called from the living room.

Emily managed a smile and the pair joined him on the sofa.

"What film?" asked Catherine.

"Something like Back to the Future."

"Good call."

Paul had the remote and searched Netflix.

"One, two or three?"

"One obviously," Emily sighed.

"Oh yeah."

The three of them watched the film with popcorn. Emily felt fidgety. She would perhaps go back to dance the day after tomorrow.

When the film was over she went upstairs with another hot chocolate. She placed it on her bedside table and noticed the hoodie had fallen off the bag with Kyle's things. She shoved it back on top, turned out the light and tried to find sleep.

The whole family, family friends, neighbours, some of Kyle's friends, Ngozi and Meg went to the beach the next day. Emily had been up early getting ready. She wore a black dress and felt uncomfortable in it. She had bought it for an elderly aunt's funeral a couple of years ago and it was no longer a good fit. She travelled in the back of her Mum's car with Ngozi and Meg. They held her hands as they had done on the way back from the shopping centre four days ago. Could it really have only been four days ago? A lifetime had passed. Emily felt as if she were entirely a different person to back then.

The cars were parked and a long line of mourners made their way down stone steps to a part of the beach that the whole family used to gather at when Emily and Kyle were little. She had fond memories of the place. She had made sand castles with her little cousin, ate ice cream with him, buried his feet in the sand. Stinging tears found their way into Emily's eyes and down her cheek.

The ashes were scattered by her weeping mother and her grief-stricken grandparents. Words of respect and remembrance were said but Emily didn't hear them.

There was a buffet back at her house. She and her friends went straight up to her room though.

"Urgh, what's this?" asked Meg.

She was standing over the bag that held Kyle's things and pointing down to it. Emily thought that she had covered it again but obviously hadn't. The hoodie was back on the floor.

"It's some of Kyle's things."

"Oh. Right," Meg said, "But what's that doing in there?"

"What?" asked Ngozi and stood up from the bed to look.

Emily joined them and saw a thick tangled mass of hair beneath some DVDs.

"Urgh," Meg said again, "Can I take it out?"

"Yeah," Emily replied, "What is it?"

"A doll I think."

Meg bent down and took out Agustinata. The dolls head lolled to one side and flopped limply in the girl's hand.

"Urgh," Meg said for a third time.

She held out the doll for Emily and Ngozi to inspect.

"Mum!" called Emily.

Catherine arrived in her room moments later.

"You ok?"

"What's that?"

Emily pointed at the doll in her friend's hand.

"I don't know," Catherine replied, "Where did you get it?"

"In the bag of Kyle's things."

Paul arrived in the room too.

"Everything ok?"

"Was that from Kyle's room?" asked Catherine.

"It was, erm, well it was in his case. It was recovered from the car."

Meg put the doll back into the bag like it was infected somehow.

"Come and join everyone downstairs, girls," Catherine said shaking away a frown.

She left the room and the others followed.

Chapter Six

FINALLY, WHEN EVERYONE HAD left, including Ngozi and Meg, Emily went back to her room. The doll was hanging from the bag. Its hair hiding its face completely. Emily lifted the doll to see what was underneath. There were mostly DVDs. There were newish titles like 'Orphan', 'The Hills Run Red' and 'Planet Terror'. She had seen these. But then there was an older looking DVD called 'Video Nasties'. She turned this over and on the back it said, "Original trailers of films that were successfully prosecuted in UK courts and deemed liable to deprave and corrupt. Some have been subsequently acquitted and removed from the DPP's list."

She shook her head. This was so like Kyle. He had probably watched this over and over again. Thirteen hours of banned movie trailers from the 1980's.

She dug deeper and found a DVD set called 'Grindhouse Trailer Classics'. There were four of them each with fifty-five movie trailers. Some of the movie titles were listed on the back such as 'Ilsa: She Wolf of the SS', 'House of Whipcord' and 'Flesh Feast'.

There was also a bulky DVD set of M R James Ghost Stories. This was more Emily's taste in film. Not the obvious slasher, horror film but rather the more subtle, spooky genre. Kyle had loved Freddy Kreuger and Jason Voorhees. She preferred The Woman in Black and The Conjuring but also films like Pan's Labyrinth and

The Ring. She liked foreign language films. They felt more realistic than Hollywood. In Hollywood films everyone was airbrushed and perfect. Everyone somehow looked amazing while running for their lives. They also made the most ridiculous and stupid decisions. Actually, she liked the Cabin in the Woods film as the director addressed exactly that. The film explored why people do these crazy things in Hollywood films.

But generally, she preferred older Hollywood films. The Amityville Horror from the 1970's was far better than the remake. She found these old 1970's and 1980's films on Netflix and some were really good. There was The Thing and Beetlejuice. They were good. The Shining, Poltergeist and The Fog. She decided she might watch a film now. Sleep was certainly far away and she might as well do something.

She delved further in the bag and found some books by Stephen King, Rob Zombie and M R Carey. He had some others that were more to her taste by Edgar Allen Poe, H P Lovecraft and M R James. She devoured those short Victorian stories and had on her own shelf less well-known writers like Arthur Machen, A N L Munby and Ben Hecht.

At the bottom of the bag was a mask. It was made from heavy black wood and looked perhaps African. It had horns like a demon. She shoved it and the doll to the bottom of the bag and buried them with the books and DVDs. Was this it? Was this all she had to remember her cousin?

Emily fell upon the bed and took out her phone. She started to flick through photos of him. Of them together.

She suddenly felt the weight of it all pushing her down. Her eyelids felt impossibly heavy and before she knew it, her phone fell from her hand. With the lights on, she fell fast asleep.

She awoke a few hours later, confused and disorientated. She looked at her clock and then at her phone to confirm the time was actually accurate. Then she turned off the light and pulled the duvet overhead.

But wait.

Was the doll that she had definitely put to the bottom of the bag now sitting on the top? She peered through the darkness at the darker shape of the bag and the still darker shape on top.

She turned the light back on.

It was.

She had put it under the books and DVDs. Hadn't she? Her mind was just not with it. Perhaps she hadn't. But either way, there was a creepy doll in her room and she was not someone in a Hollywood film. She pushed the duvet to one side and pushed the sliding door of her wardrobe open. Her eyes scanned the clothes pushed and shoved here and there but eventually saw a shoe box under a few leotards. She pulled it free and tipped the trainers onto the floor. Then the doll was placed inside. The box reminded her of a little coffin. She shook free the thought and put the lid back on. The box was then pushed to the back of the bottom of the wardrobe under shoes and the doors were firmly closed.

Emily climbed back into bed and turned off the light. Should she do the same with the mask too? That was still in the bag though. Only the doll had moved. Well, not moved, but seemed to be not where she had first put it.

She tried to find sleep but her thoughts kept buzzing around keeping her awake. Thoughts of Kyle. She imagined him in that car. The terror of it all.

But despite the best efforts from her brain to keep her awake, sleep finally found her again.

In the dark and silent room Emily awoke to the sound of crying. Her brow furrowed. Was she imagining it? Was it herself crying?

She sat up and looked at her clock. The illuminated display read three thirty-three AM. She turned on the light and the crying stopped.

It must have been her imagination. She was under a lot of stress. Stress was a killer, her grandad always said.

At least she didn't have to go to school. She couldn't have done that. She went downstairs to get a glass of water. Her Mum and Paul were asleep. Well, Paul was anyway. She could hear him snoring. Her Mum would tell him off in the morning over coffee.

It was fortunate to be the school holidays at least. At school everyone would have been talking about Kyle. Probably whispering about her behind her back. Probably scrutinising her every word and movement. She imagined various scenarios. The school holidays would not be long enough though. Would she be able to go back in October rather than September?

She poured the water and drank a full glass. She refilled it and stumbled in the darkness back up the stairs. She reached for her bedroom door but as she grabbed it, the door slammed closed.

She paused. She remained standing there holding the water and looking at the gloomy white wood.

She definitely had hold of the door handle but it been yanked out of her hand. Slowly, she reached for the handle again. She turned it and opened the door. It was like she was moving under water; all her actions were in slow motion. Her feet stayed fixed on the carpet of the landing. The light from her room spilled into the dark all around her. She leaned in and peered into her room. All was as she had left it. The first place she looked was her wardrobe doors. They were thankfully still closed.

She scanned the rest of the room. Everything was fine.

It had been her imagination and nothing more.

Letting out a long sigh, she stepped toward her bed. She had another gulp of water and climbed under the duvet. She flicked off the light and tried to sleep but she just couldn't. After persisting for a while longer she finally decided to watch a film on her iPad. Netflix recommended films like Hellraiser and Thirty Days of Night even Cult of Chucky, but Emily didn't want to watch anything like that. She finally decided upon The Iron Giant. She had loved that film when she was little and found comfort in the animation.

When it was over, she could hear her Mum making morning coffee. She slid from beneath the duvet and joined her in the kitchen.

"How'd you sleep?" her Mum asked cheerily.

Emily shrugged,

"You?"

"Hmm, not great."

"I could hear him."

"Did he keep you awake too?"

Her Mum looked angry and defensive. Emily smiled.

"No. It wasn't him."

Her Mum then looked sad. She looked down and nodded.

"What do you want to do about dance later?" she asked at last, "You want to go?"

"Yeah I do."

Emily looked to one side as if the decision had only just occurred to her. She nodded as if to confirm it to herself. She did want to dance. She could lose herself in it.

"Let's go to Frankie and Benny's for breakfast," her Mum said smiling.

Emily furrowed her brow.

"I'm not hungry."

Her Mum nodded and mouthed but didn't say 'ok'.

"Hot chocolate?"

Emily returned the nod and smiled.

"I'll take it up and get a shower."

Her Mum gave her a brief hug.

"Are you ok?"

Her Mum shrugged. She had lost a sister. But not only a sister, a best friend. Emily hugged her again.

"We'll get through this," she whispered to her Mum.

"I know," she replied, "We have to."

Emily took her hot chocolate upstairs then showered. She washed and conditioned her thick hair. She stood under the heavy flow of the water. The room filled with steam. She then sat in the bath and just let the warm water envelope her. It was comforting and she needed its warm embrace.

After several minutes she finally turned off the taps and took the towel. She wrapped it around herself and went to her room. She dried herself and put on a dressing gown. She was hot and finished the water from last night then went back downstairs for more. She could never remember being so thirsty.

Her Mum was ironing and smiled at her but said nothing. Emily took the glass of water back upstairs and to her room. She plugged in her hair dryer and straighteners. Her Mum's hair dryer was much better but she didn't want to wake Paul.

She looked for her brush but realised she must have left it in the bathroom when she went to bed last night. She went to collect it but then stopped as soon as she entered the room. Something was written on the mirror. A single word on the steamed glass.

Written with in small letters but unmistakably there. Casa.

Casa? What did it mean? She had heard the expression 'mi casa es tu casa', which she thought meant 'my home is your home'. So, casa meant home. Home?

Why would Paul write that on the mirror? Was he even up? She wiped the word with her hand. Maybe he had written it last night and it had only just appeared now in the steam from the shower. Home wasn't a sinister word. It was something that was perhaps meant to comfort you. But it didn't offer any comfort when written on a mirror. She hadn't noticed it before when she had been in the bathroom just now. Was she losing her mind?

Stressed out. She was stressed out with everything that had happened and that was all. She didn't need to be intense about silly things. Weird stuff happens all of the time and that was that. Dwelling on every little thing would get you nowhere.

She left the bathroom with the brush then dried her hair and got dressed. She messaged Ngozi and Meg to come over whenever they were up. She would hang out with them then go to dance later. There was no reason to freak out about a word on a mirror or a door closing or hearing crying.

But she would get rid of that doll though. She didn't want it. It wasn't like she had even heard Kyle mention it before. Was that what he had brought back from his holiday? Was that the thing he had messaged her about?

She would keep the books and DVDs, maybe even the mask, but she didn't want the doll. She just didn't.

Not that she thought it was haunted or anything but rather she just didn't like the thing. As she told herself last night, she was not in a Hollywood film. She was not being directed by anyone. She could make her own choices and decisions. She found the doll creepy and so she would get rid of it. Simple as that.

Chapter Seven

NGOZI ARRIVED AROUND TEN AM. They were sitting in Emily's room on their phones.

"Where's Meg?" asked Ngozi.

"She's not coming," Emily replied, looking up from her phone, "She said she had family stuff on."

Ngozi nodded.

"Did you get to sleep last night?"

Emily shook her head.

"Weird stuff happened."

She told her friend about the word on the mirror she saw, the door she had felt and the crying she had heard. She lifted the box down from the wardrobe and took off the lid. The huge hair framed the glowing white face. The lifeless eyes looked up at the two girls. It was like they were viewing a corpse in a coffin. A tiny, dead, baby girl.

Ngozi shuddered.

"What you want to do with it?"

Emily sighed,

"I know it belonged to Kyle but I'm getting rid of it."

Ngozi nodded,

"I would too."

"How do you think I should do it? I can't just put it in the bin, can I?"

"Hmm," Ngozi rubbed her chin thoughtfully, "What about the bin outside of the Co-op?"

"What if someone finds it? I don't want it but I don't really want anyone else to have it either. I don't know why, I just don't."

"Fair enough. I understand. It was Kyle's after all."

Emily sighed again, louder this time,

"You think I should keep it, don't you?'

"Nah, it's not that. It's just . . . you're right. I mean how can you just put it in the bin? You could burn it maybe? Hasn't Paul got a wood burning thing in the garden?"

"I can't burn it."

Emily made a groaning sound and fell backwards onto the bed.

Ngozi laughed and tickled her stomach. Emily laughed and slapped away her friend's hands.

"Let's just go and do something," Ngozi said, "Leave that thing in the box and let's go into town."

Emily sat up, nodding. She then stood up while putting the lid back on the box and pushed it back into the wardrobe.

"Shops in town are rubbish though," she sighed over her shoulder, "Maybe we should take the bus to Newcastle."

"Ok," Ngozi nodded, "Then stay at mine tonight and forget about everything."

Emily smiled.

"Sounds like an actual plan and everything."

The pair went off and waited an age for the bus. Emily felt normality creeping in and relaxed for the first time since Kyle's death. She didn't buy anything but helped Ngozi choose a few things.

They got a lift back after Ngozi's Dad finished work. He wordlessly drove them down the motorway as a huge storm erupted. The sky was vast and drenched in gun metal grey. It growled and the earth below trembled. It was vast and powerful to remind all those below of their own unimportance and immortality. When the rumbling clouds released huge blobs of raindrops that thudded enormously on the metal roof of the car then Ngozi's Dad slowed right down. The car slid slowly through the gigantic puddles that were forming on the tarmac.

"We don't have to go *this* slowly, Reggie."

Ngozi always called her Dad Reggie. It wasn't his real name. His real name was Thomas. Emily always found this amusing and strange. Paul was her step Dad, sort of, and to call him Paul was natural. But Ngozi didn't call her real Dad but by another name. Reggie, Thomas, whatever. It just meant that Emily never knew how to address him. She usually tried not to but if she felt a name was necessary then she generally went for Reggie.

Emily looked out of the window. The rain had turned to hail. It hammered the landscape loudly. The weather was so unpredictable right now. It had been boiling for days and now this.

The rhythmic tap tap tapping somehow soothed her and she sat back in the car watching Ngozi and Reggie bicker. She couldn't hear their words but smiled at the playful banter bouncing back and forth as the car was bombarded with falling ice in a humid atmosphere.

Emily texted her Mum to say she was staying at Ngozi's and would be missing dance. To miss dance was unusual but everyone would be fine with it. Staying out for the night was not unusual though. She stayed at Ngozi's or Meg's a lot or they stayed with her. She used her friend's toothbrushes and makeup remover on a night. Then she used the toothbrush again in the morning along with their makeup and deodorant.

A night away would do her the world of good.

And it did.

The next morning, Emily ate some cereal then thanked Ngozi's Mum, Asha. Reggie had already gone to work earlier. Emily and Ngozi hugged then she was off. She walked back toward home. It was only fifteen minutes but Emily wished it was longer. She thought she might take the more scenic route but didn't in the end. If was early morning yet the heat was stifling. She looked at her watch. It read three thirty-three AM. It had stopped. Hadn't that been the time she had woken the night before?

She checked her phone for the real time and adjusted her watch accordingly. The wind whipped up around her. A hot, warm wind, almost tropical even.

She arrived home and no one was in. She used her keys and found a note on the kitchen bench. Who left notes? It made her laugh out loud to the empty house. 'Gone to work. I'll be home around five. Paul might be back earlier. There's chili and rice in the fridge. Mum xxx.'

A note. Honestly, Emily knew of no one else on the planet who still left notes. Her Mum was so funny. It was like she was stuck in the 1990's.

She shook her head and walked up the stairs. Her room smelt of clean washing and she smiled. But then the smile fell. On her bed was the doll. It was laid upon the duvet with its head resting upon a pillow. Its cold eyes looked lifelessly skyward.

"What the hell?"

Her bed had been changed. The crisp white duvet was smooth like glass. The fabric conditioner smell filled the room. Everything had been tidied and dusted. The floor was vacuumed. The doll was rigid.

Why would her Mum do such a thing? Why would she go into her wardrobe, find the doll inside a box and then place it upon the bed? What would make her do such a thing?

She shook her head angrily, grabbed the doll and tossed it back into the trainer box. She then shoved it back into the wardrobe and pilled clothes messily on top.

Looking at the clean bed, it was like the doll had somehow infected it with invisible dirt and Emily didn't want to lie down where the doll had been.

Perhaps she would bin the doll after all. Perhaps she would burn it or bury it. But by burning she would be cremating, like what had happened to Kyle. By burying it then it made it more like a real person. Where would she bury it anyway? In the garden? It would always be there for her. When was bin day? Paul kept a timetable stuck inside a kitchen cupboard. She would check it and on bin day she would get rid of it.

Her room was her place of solace and now it had been spoiled somehow. She knew she was being ridiculous but perhaps her grief over Kyle was being manifested upon this doll.

She knew it was just a thing. But she didn't want it in her room. She pushed the duvet to one side and laid upon the bed. She had two pillows and she used the one that the doll had not been touching.

Her eyes scanned her room and she breathed in deeply. A square canvas featuring the Eiffel Tower was on the wall to her right. There were also shelves there that held her dance trophies and medals. On her left were the sliding doors of the wardrobes that held the . . . box. Straight ahead were the windows framed by thick curtains and black out liners. Next to her bed was her dressing table. Her perfume, makeup, hair brushes, makeup brushes, mirror and other cosmetics were all there. This was her domain. Everything was as it should be, except for one thing.

She sighed, got up and went downstairs to check the bin collection timetable. Looking at her phone to check the date, she then checked the timetable. Wait, this was for the garden bin. Where was the normal bin timetable? There wasn't one.

She would have to ask Paul when he got in from work.

Emily went back upstairs to collect her iPad and Beats headphones. She usually watched Netflix in her room but she decided to curl up onto the sofa today. She might text Meg and ask if she was free that night. Her eyes scanned her room and saw that her Mum had put her iPad on her dressing table. The Beats were folded next to it. Then she saw a thin crack in her mirror.

It was hadn't been there a moment ago.

Had it?

It was a single line that ran diagonally over the entire surface of the glass. She couldn't have missed it just now.

Could she?

She groaned. Paul would be so grumpy about replacing it. It was an Ikea set so not expensive but she had only just got it.

Leaning closer, she peered at it. As if inspecting it would somehow heal the wounded glass. It was then she noticed her bedside clock. It read three thirty-three AM.

She left the room at once. What was going on? She felt cold and alone. She went downstairs but then back up again to collect her iPad. Instead of opening Netflix she opened Safari instead. Then she googled 'what does 3 33 am mean?'.

The answers varied from guardian angels reminding you about the Holy Trinity to a demonic sign of impending death. She scanned a few contradictory websites then gave up. She slapped the iPad cover over the screen and sighed into the sofa.

Perhaps her watch stopping and her clock stopping at exactly the same time were a mad coincidence. These things happened in the world. Perhaps her Mum had put the doll on her bed for some mental 'typical-mum' reason.

But, her mirror had been cracked. There was no denying the reality of that. She had not done it. If her Mum had done then there would have been a 'mum-note'. Maybe Paul had done it but he didn't really ever go into her room except to deliver food and drink or to build something for her.

It was just so stupid to blame the doll. It was just so ridiculous. Yet she did.

Emily then stood up. She wore a determined frown. She marched up the stairs and took the box from the wardrobe. It was blue with the three distinctive white Adidas lines running around it. She lifted the lid slightly to check the doll was still inside. Of course it was. What was wrong with her?

She thudded down the stairs and went into the kitchen. She pressed the lid of the bin and it gaped wide open, ready to be fed. It was half full. Half empty? Kitchen roll and the contents of the vacuum cleaner sat upon scraped food scraps and packaging. She plunged her hand beneath the waste and pushed everything to one side. She then pushed the box to the bottom. There was barely enough room. She covered the box with the contents of the bin and closed the lid. It was full to the brim.

Emily turned on the tap and washed thoroughly with soap and hot water. Then she went back to the bin and took off the lid. She tied the liner closed and pulled free the bag. With a heavy thud she dropped it into the wheelie bin outside.

She had done it. The doll was gone.

Chapter Eight

EMILY SPENT THE REMAINDER of the afternoon watching Netflix. She stayed away from the horror genre and stuck to episodes of Friends and The Big Bang Theory that she had seen before. Her thoughts frequently returned to the doll though. The wheelie bin had been empty suggesting that the rubbish wouldn't be taken for a while. The doll would sit there for up to two weeks.

It didn't matter. What was it going to do? Climb out and break into the house? To do what? Write a word and break a mirror? She laughed at herself. It was forced and false though.

The house felt empty and she felt alone. She looked at her phone. Why hadn't Meg replied to her text she had sent? She texted Ngozi and asked what she was doing. Ngozi replied and said she was helping her Mum cook. Emily asked if she could come over and the reply beeped in 'yeah' with a high-pitched urgency.

She slid off the bed and brushed her hair roughly. Then she grabbed her keys, phone and purse. She shoved them in a bag, slung it over her shoulder and was off. Ngozi lived only a few streets away. The way the housing estate they lived on was structured, it was actually quicker to walk there than drive, not that she could drive, yet.

After locking the house, Emily was off down the street, down some steps, left turns and one right then she was there.

The outside of Ngozi's house was pristine. There was a thick, lush hanging basket with a myriad of colours. A perfectly pruned bush sat beside the front door like a friendly, welcoming guard.

She pressed the doorbell which chimed in a high pitched yet relaxed voice. The porch was decorated with shoes that sat in rigid straight lines. Soldiers of leather or suede.

Ngozi's Mum came to the door with a huge smile.

"Emily!" she beamed.

"Hi Asha," Emily smiled back.

Asha grabbed her and hugged her then literally dragged the girl into the house. Emily laughed as she was taken into the kitchen. The smell of peanuts, spices and cooked meat hung thickly in the air. Ngozi was stood beside Reggie chopping and slicing at the worktop. He was home very early but this wasn't unusual.

"Hey," she called over her shoulder.

"Grab a knife," Reggie said without looking up, "You're on Waakye."

Emily smiled and nodded. She had both made and eaten this before at Ngozi's house. It was rice and beans but Reggie made his with lots of spices.

Without waiting to be shown or asked she took a sieve from a corner cupboard and then a massive bag of rice from the garage. She washed the rice thoroughly then added a tin of beans. While the rice and beans were sitting under a cold tap she flicked on the kettle. The spices were already out. She peeled and chopped an onion, added stock and oil then fried these in a pan. She added the spice and asked,

"What spices are we using Reggie?"

He was chopping chicken and waved his knife menacingly at her,

"If I tell you then I'll have to kill you!"

She smiled and he laughed. It was something he had said to her many times before. Emily never cooked at home but always joined in with the family cooking at Ngozi's house. They made big batches of things together and froze portions in plastic tubs for easy meals later.

"What are you making?"

Ngozi looked up and furrowed her brow.

"What meat is this Reggie?" she asked her Dad.

"Crocodile," he laughed back.

Ngozi groaned and looked at Emily.

"It's chicken and peanut soup."

"If you know then why did you ask?" Reggie yelled.

"To see what ridiculous answer you'll give the girl," snapped Asha.

She was chopping plantains.

"Are you making red-red?" asked Emily.

"Yes, your favourite."

Emily blushed a little. Ngozi's family always said that red-red was her favourite because of her hair. It wasn't her favourite. She found it a bit tasteless but she always went along with it.

Ngozi's little brother, Adisa, was peeling avocados and staring up at Emily. This was not unusual. She looked at him and though he ordinarily looked away, this time he didn't. He smiled at her.

The smile was meant to express comfort but all it did was brought the memory of Kyle back to her in a tidal wave of grief. She fought back the sting of tears and concentrated on stirring the rice and beans in the pan she held.

After another ten minutes had passed, Emily shook her head and returned to the kitchen.

Reggie was dancing with Asha and Adisa looked embarrassed. Ngozi put her hand on Emily's shoulder.

"You ok?"

"Yeah, I put the doll in the bin."

Ngozi started laughing. Emily looked at her for a few moments and then laughed too.

"You heard from Meg?"

"Yeah," Ngozi replied, still laughing, "She messaged me this morning."

"She hasn't replied to mine."

"She will."

The food was taken to the table. Everyone sat down and helped themselves. Emily poured the chicken and peanut soup over her Waakye. She added a little red-red out of politeness but mixed it with mashed avocado for flavour. There were some green leafy vegetables, some she knew, others she didn't.

Reggie talked and talked. He described scenes from his home in Accra.

"My family is related to royalty," he was saying, "I have blue blood in my veins."

"You have a distant cousin, third removed," Asha said shaking her head, "Don't exaggerate."

"We're a close family! There are no distant cousins!"

The food was richly mixed with stories and laughter. It was exactly what Emily needed. By the early evening, she felt refreshed and relaxed. Her Mum had texted asking where she was. She eventually replied saying that she would be home soon. But perhaps she wouldn't. Perhaps she would stay right there with Ngozi and her family again.

Why? She told herself it was to be away from the grief-stricken house and family. But that wasn't true. It was the thought of that doll sitting outside. It just gave her the creeps. She firmly told herself that she was being ridiculous and told Ngozi that she had to go home soon.

Later, she hugged Ngozi, Reggie and Asha. She gave Adisa a little wave and he looked embarrassed as he smiled back at her shyly.

Emily walked slowly back the same way she had come. But then she deviated, taking a longer route. The sky brooded darkly above her. Vast dark clouds were gathering. It was still hot though. The air felt tropical and heavy. There was a damp, humid taste in the air.

Eventually, she walked through the front door concentrating hard on not looking at the large black bin down the side of the house.

"Hi," she called when she stepped inside.

Paul and her Mum were cooking in the kitchen.

"Have you eaten?" he asked.

"Yeah, at Ngozi's."

"You ok?" her Mum asked.

Emily nodded, gave her a brief hug then went upstairs. She sat on her bed and looked out of the window. The storm continued to grow and darkness enveloped the sky.

She walked over to the window and looked down at the row of three wheelie bins to the right of her house. Then she closed the curtains and lay down upon her bed. She put in her Beats and watched her iPad while simultaneously checking Snapchat and Instagram.

Hours passed in this way until her Mum was knocking on her door. She opened it slowly. She looked as if she'd been crying and had definitely been drinking. She wobbled slightly as she peered round the door. Emily closed her iPad and pulled the Beats down around her neck.

"I'm going to bed," her Mum said, "You want anything."

"No, I'm good."

"OK, good night. I love you."

"Love you too."

Her Mum closed the door and Emily heard the light go out on the landing and her Mum's bedroom door close too.

After a while, the house was silent and still. Emily finally put her headphones back on but soon felt sleepy. She put out her bedside light and soon drifted into a light sleep as thunder rumbled somewhere in the distance.

Emily's eyes snapped wide open in the darkness. She sat up. A massive clap of thunder had woken her. She looked at her clock hoping it wouldn't be three thirty-three was it was. The red numbers glowed viciously. It was.

She groaned and shook her head. She turned over, with her back to the clock and wrapped the pillow over her ears. There was another loud clap of thunder and the whole house shook. She felt her bed move. The storm must have been right above her room. She tried to find sleep but it was impossible.

She sighed as she sat up. Not wanting to, she found herself walking to her window. The curtains were pulled back and there was a flash of lightning in the sky. She was about to start counting to see how far away the storm was but the sound of thunder came in less than a second.

"It really is above the house," she said out loud.

Then she saw it. Illuminated by the light of the storm for the briefest moment. It was the doll. It was laid out on the driveway beneath her window. But, no. It couldn't have been. There was darkness now and she couldn't see it any longer. It had been her imagination. It had to have been.

Another flash of light cracked across the sky. The doll was there again. Only it had moved. It was now standing, *standing* on the drive. Her mind was a tangled mess of thoughts. They jostled for primary position. They rose and fell at tremendous speed. Her brain could not process this. Her mouth was wide open and her eyes were bulging. Goosebumps prickled her flesh all over. She felt hot and cold at once.

More lightning lit up the sky and now the doll had its head lifted and was looking at her. It was looking up at the window. Its black eyes staring blankly without any hint of emotion at all.

This could not be happening. It was a dream. It was her imagination. It was a trick of the light. It was not real. But it was.

With another bolt from the sky the doll held out its arms. With another it was moving toward the house. Each flash of light showed its movements. Toward the front door. Toward her.

Locked legs imprisoned her body. She could not move. She could not look away. She didn't want to see this, this impossible scene.

Then, at last, she did move. She sprinted away from the window and hurled herself out of her room. She burst into her Mum's room and fell upon the bed. Paul sat up and her Mum shrieked in alarm.

"What's wrong?" Paul asked, turning on the bedside lamp.

Emily made some hysterical noises that made no sense. She was babbling and crying but couldn't get her words out in the right order. Her Mum was holding her and Emily sobbed into her.

"It's ok," her Mum was saying, "Its ok. I know. I know. Just let it all out."

Emily turned to look at the door. She was expecting the doll to be there but thankfully it was not.

"Outside!" she almost shrieked, "There was . . . something outside! Trying to get in!"

Paul was up. He kept a huge Maglite torch next to his bedside table. He had been told by a friend that if an intruder came in the house, the best weapon was one these torches. They were heavy and could be used like a baseball bat. But use a baseball bat and you can be prosecuted.

He stumbled over toward the door brandishing the torch.

"No, don't," Emily was saying, "Don't!"

Her Mum held her tightly and Paul went door the stairs. Emily heard the keys in the lock being turned. He was going outside. Outside to the doll.

Chapter Nine

EMILY WAS SOBBING AND shaking her head. She was waiting for Paul's screams to echo up the stairs. But nothing came. Her Mum kept whispering that everything was going to be ok and stroking her hair and back. Emily's eyes were wide and unblinking. Her wild, shocked expression was fixed. She held her breath.

Then, he was back.

"I couldn't see anything," he said, "There was no sign of anyone out there."

Emily stared at him. Her sweat drenched hair was plastered over her forehead.

"You didn't see anything on the drive? There was nothing there at all?"

She became aware that she wasn't using the word 'doll'. Her hysterical mind began to try and make sense of what had just happened.

She'd been asleep. It could have been the remnants of a dream. The light from the storm was something that could disorientate. She was grieving for Kyle. It hadn't happened. That was why she didn't say she had seen the doll.

But a tiny part of her knew that it had happened.

Paul sat on the bed and stroked Emily's back while her Mum hugged her. It had all seemed so real and yet unreal at the same time. She closed her eyes and saw the doll's face vividly looking up at her from outside. The wild wind whipped its hair up into the air. Its black eyes bore into her. Its white face glowed like the moon. The red lips were a slashed scar.

She opened her eyes and moaned softly.

"Sleep here," Paul said, "Or try to. I'll go in the other room."

He left them there and her Mum told her to get under the covers. Emily did but knew it was pointless. She didn't think she would sleep ever again but then she did. Sleep enveloped her. She didn't dream, or at least she couldn't remember dreaming. Thankfully, she had no nightmares. No visions of dolls or of anything at all.

When morning arrived, she actually felt pretty good. She heard the sounds of her Mum making hot chocolate in the microwave. She heard Paul getting ready for work.

Emily sat up and firmly told herself that last night was the result of stress, grief and exhaustion. She'd had another short but good night's sleep and would just do *normal* stuff today. Then she would dance tonight and sleep in her bed.

Everything would be fine.

But the haunting image of the doll looking up at her still hung around the edges of her mind. She tried to use positive thinking to exorcise it completely but it was still there.

She ignored it and went downstairs.

"Morning," Paul said, acting like last night hadn't happened.

"Morning," her Mum beamed at her, "What you doing today?"

Emily smiled back at them.

"Morning," she replied, "Think I'll see Ngozi and Meg and then dance tonight."

She decided to join in with the charade of pretending too. Taking out her phone, she checked up on Snapchat and Instagram then messaged her friends.

Ngozi replied straight away but her messages to Meg looked to be unread. On Instagram it said that she had been active six hours ago but yet she had not replied to Emily.

She shook her head. It was up to Meg she supposed. Maybe there was something going on. Meg lived with her Mum and two brothers and there was usually some drama. She never saw her Dad but there had been a bad time when he had tried to make contact.

Her phone vibrated and Emily saw that Ngozi had replied with 'I'll come round in a bit'. She checked Meg's status again and shrugged.

Emily's Mum then handed her a croissant and a hot chocolate.

"I'd better get ready for work," she said, "You sure you're ok today?"

The 'today' part clearly was in reference to 'last night' but no one was talking about that.

"Yeah," Emily smiled, "I'm fine."

"You sure?" asked Paul.

"Go, go."

The pair nodded and went upstairs leaving Emily to her breakfast and phone. She looked out of the window. Large candy floss white clouds filled the brilliant blue above. The sky was at such a stark contrast to the storm the night before. She smiled. Her mind was that sky today. She felt so different to yesterday.

She skipped up the stairs, showered, washed her hair and started to get ready for the day.

Her phone vibrated on her dressing table. She wondered if it would be Meg. It was Ngozi saying 'Liam has asked if we want to meet him and a few others outside McDonalds tonight'.

Emily rolled her eyes and groaned. She found Liam so annoying. He was such a show off and Ngozi changed when she was around him. She joined in calling Emily her 'ginger mate'. She hung on his every word and laughed too loudly at his stupid jokes. His posts on Instagram were always with his top off.

'Ive got dance', she sent back.

'miss it.'

'cant. got an exam coming up.'

'loser.'

'u know it.'

'see ya in a bit.'

'30 min.'

She borrowed her Mum's Dyson hair dryer and GHD straighteners. Her Mum followed her into her room to hug her goodbye. Paul shouted his goodbye up the stairs.

Emily slid skinny blue jeans on and shoved her phone into her back pocket. She pulled a blue Calvin Klein T shirt on and went down stairs. After pushing her feet into a pair of white Air Max 97's, she set off. Walking slowly, she felt the sunshine on her skin and a slight breeze flicked up her hair. She smiled.

When she arrived at Ngozi's, she knocked at the door. Reggie's car was gone but her Mum's was still on the drive.

Adisa opened the door and said 'hello' in a voice rather deeper than his usual. It sounded rehearsed and Emily almost laughed.

"Hi," she said brightly and walked past him.

After she took off her shoes, she hugged Asha and went up the stairs. Ngozi was laid upon her bed looking at her laptop, watching Netflix.

"What's up?"

"Not much," smiled Emily, "Hey you heard from Meg? She's like not returning any of my messages."

"Yeah, I heard this morning."

"That's so weird. I'll call her now."

Emily Facetimed Meg but there was no reply.

"You try," she said to Ngozi.

She did and Meg's face appeared on her MacBook.

"Hi," Meg's face filled the laptop screen, "What you doing?"

Emily joined Ngozi on the bed.

"Oh, erm, yeah, erm, hi Emily."

"What's going on?"

"Erm, nothing."

There was an awkward silence that lasted a few seconds but felt like forever. Finally Meg broke it and said,

"I – I , tell you what, I'm coming over."

The call was ended and the screen went back to Netflix. Morty was paused mid panic.

"That was weird," Ngozi said, frowning.

"Has she been ok with you?"

"Totally."

"She's been completely ignoring me."

"Hmm, guess we'll find out why soon."

Emily nodded and laid on her stomach facing the MacBook screen.

"Put it back on," she said to Ngozi, "I've seen this one anyway."

Ngozi pressed the spacebar and Morty shrieked and shouted nonsensically. Half way through the next episode Meg arrived in the room. Emily sat up.

Meg normally had her incredibly long blonde hair straightened to perfection. Her foundation and mascara was always immaculate but she had clearly got here in a hurry.

"I'm so sorry, Emily."

Meg hugged her.

"It's ok," Emily said, "I've just been worried. Are you ok?"

Meg bit her lip and sat on the bed.

"It's just with Kyle . . . "

"Yeah?" Emily asked.

"And the funeral. I just . . . I just couldn't handle it all. I'm mean he's dead. He's really dead."

Ngozi let out a long sigh.

"Are you for real?"

"I know it's selfish. I know I'm meant to be there for you. I just thought I'd make it all worse if I couldn't get my shit together."

"Meg, seriously," Ngozi said firmly, "It was *her* cousin."

"It's ok," Emily smiled warmly at them both, "I totally understand. But really who can get their shit together over this?"

The three nodded and chatted for a long time. The conversation quickly moved from Kyle to celebrity gossip and then on to gossip about people from school. They showed each other photos of posts people had made. They Snapchatted throughout too.

Then Ngozi suddenly sat up.

"Hey! I've just remembered. Tell Meg about the doll!"

Emily's face fell.

"Has something else happened?" asked Ngozi a little too excitedly.

"That creepy thing I pulled out of Kyle's bag?"

Emily nodded slowly.

"She put it in the wheelie bin outside!" Ngozi laughed.

"I'm going to tell you both something," Emily began seriously, "But you have to promise me you won't tell anyone."

Her friends nodded solemnly. Their eyes wide and mouths closed.

"Last night something really weird happened. I think I imagined it all. Really, I do. I mean it would be ridiculous to think anything else. After all, my shit is the least together in this room. I mean it."

"What happened?" whispered Ngozi.

"You know the storm we had?"

The pair nodded.

"Well it woke me up at three thirty-three."

Meg gasped.

"There's loads of stuff on YouTube about three thirty-three!"

"I know. I've been waking up at that time every night since it happened. Since Kyle died."

"Do you think his ghost is waking you?" Meg asked, "Do you think he's trying to contact you?"

Emily furrowed her brow. She shook her head no.

Ngozi nodded for Emily to go on.

"I went to the window and in the storm, I thought I saw the doll standing on the drive."

"No way!" Ngozi hissed. "Just, like, standing there?"

"Well sort of. Then it moved. Like, by itself."

"What?" Meg asked.

"Yeah it was moving. Toward me."

"What did you do?"

"I ran to my Mum's room. Paul went downstairs to check if everything was ok. He said there was nothing there."

"Did you tell them you saw the doll?" Ngozi asked.

"No way," Emily snorted, "They'd have me off to the doctors for a head check. I told them I saw someone."

"Where's the doll now?" asked Meg.

"Still in the bin outside, I guess."

"What, it got back in?"

"Well, no" Emily laughed, "It didn't happen in the first place, did it? I imagined it obviously."

The three girls said nothing. But then Emily added,

"There's been other stuff too though. Creepy stuff."

"Like what?" Meg leaned closer as she asked this.

"Well, I put the doll in a box in my wardrobe but then I found it on my bed. I just guessed Paul or Mum had done it."

"Have you asked them?"

"No, it felt weird. But that's why I put it in the bin."

"You can stay here tonight if you like?" Ngozi suggested.

"Thanks, but I can't just stay at yours just 'cause I'm scared of a doll in the bin."

The three of them laughed at this.

"Yeah but I wouldn't want to sleep in the house, you know." Meg eventually said. "We should get rid of it."

"Get rid of it? How?"

Emily brow was creased. Ngozi was nodding.

"Yeah, she's right. Let's take it somewhere."

"What? Put it in a public bin? Up the big bins at Lidl or somewhere? I've thought about that. I just can't do it. Someone might find it. And it was Kyle's."

"Well then let's bury is somewhere." Meg suggested.

"We could give it a funeral," Ngozi said but then regretted the words as soon as they were out of her mouth.

She winced slightly.

"Sorry," she whispered.

"I think that might be the best answer actually," Emily said thoughtfully, "Yeah. That feels right. I don't want it in the house. I don't want it in a bin. Let's give it a burial."

Chapter Ten

"Where shall we bury it though?" asked Ngozi.

All three girls furrowed their brows in thought.

"The nature reserve?" Emily suggested.

They nodded as one and stood up. Ngozi grabbed a backpack from her wardrobe.

"My parents are out so we can get shovels and whatever else we need from mine." Emily said.

"Shovels?" laughed Meg, "It's only a doll."

"OK, then. A small digging thing, a trowel or whatever it's called."

They went down the stairs and Ngozi shouted,

"We're going out, Mum and Asha!"

"Text me later," her Mum shouted back from the kitchen, "I need to know how many I'm feeding today!"

"Will do," Ngozi replied.

"Bye!" Meg shouted.

"Bye!" added Emily.

The trio walked chatting enthusiastically about the doll until they reached Emily's street. Then a kind of strange silence settled. They approached the front door and Emily said,

"Let's get the stuff we need first."

"Why not check its actually in the bin first?" Ngozi suggested.

"Why wouldn't it be in the bin?" Emily snapped back, "You think it really did get out and looked up at me last night?"

Meg was walking toward the black bin to the left of the house.

"Meg, wait," Emily protested.

But Meg was right next to it. She turned to look at her friends. Then she slowly, perhaps nervously, lifted the lid. Flies buzzed around her. There was a lot of them. They buzzed viciously about her hair. She swatted them a few times but then gave up and lifted the lid with one swift movement that made it thud against the side.

She peered in but could not see the doll. Turning to her friends she made a shrugging motion.

"Look under the top bin bag," suggested Ngozi, "It might be under that."

More flies manically swarmed about her as she lifted up a limp black bag.

There it was.

The lid was off the box and the doll in the black dress lay slumped beneath the bin bag. Had someone put a bag on top of it? Had Catherine or Paul seen the doll but just ignored it? Had they not seen it at all? These were the questions that fizzed inside all three of the girl's minds as all three now peered into the bin.

Meg dropped the bag on top of the doll.

"Let's get what we need then," she said.

The others nodded and they walked, single file down the other side of the house to the back garden and the shed. Emily remembered she only had one key. She found carrying too many keys was so annoying.

She told the others to wait, went back to the front of the house, without looking at the wheelie bin and went inside. She collected the shed key and unlocked the back door. The three went into the shed and collected two trowels, a hand garden fork and a weird three-pronged claw thing.

They stuffed all of these into Ngozi's backpack and locked the shed. They went in through the back door of the house and locked that too. As they walked through Emily's house Meg stopped,

"You think it's still going to be there?"

The others stopped too.

They looked at each other. They slowly walked to the front door, opened it and stepped onto the drive. They each craned their necks to look at the bin by the side of the house. The lid tap tap tapped against the side of the bin in a rhythmic beat in a slight wind. It matched Emily's heart thumping in her chest.

They walked forward and peered into bin. The doll was underneath the bag. They shoved this to one side. The doll was still staring with unblinking eyes up at the sky.

"Phew!" laughed Meg.

All three then laughed.

"Urgh," Ngozi said as she picked the box that held the doll, "It stinks."

Angry flies swarmed all around the box. Emily reached in and grabbed the doll by its body. The black dress with white frills on the collar and neck rustled in her hand. The raven black hair fell downward and the head lolled to one side.

Ngozi opened the backpack and Emily dropped the doll in like it was a snake or some such other poisonous creature. The three of them peered inside the bag. The doll's white face looked up at them. It seemed to glow in the gloom of the back. The blue eyes looked black. The garden tools looked sinister next to the tiny white hands.

Ngozi zipped the bag shut and slung it over one shoulder.

"Let's go then," she said and set off.

The others followed. The tools rattled as they walked. No one spoke at first but the noise from the bag made them uncomfortable so eventually Ngozi said,

"Reggie keeps going on about some road being built through the nature reserve. He does my head in about it."

"Why do you call him Reggie?" asked Meg, "I've always meant to ask."

"It's not his real name you know," Ngozi laughed.

"I knew that but I've never asked why do you call him that?" Emily smiled, "What's his real name again? Thomas?"

"Yeah, his real name is Thomas but everyone calls him Reggie. It was my first word and it just sort of stuck from there."

"Does Adisa call him Reggie?"

"Yeah, you not noticed?"

"Not really."

The three chatted about their families for a while as they entered the nature reserve. The stormy nights and sunny days had made the whole place incredibly overgrown. The path was almost entirely devoured by the trees and bushes but also a huge number of nettles. The girls walked in single file. Ngozi had the backpack in her hands and was pushing through the nettles with it.

"Ow," Meg kept saying.

"I know, I've been stung about a million times," moaned Emily.

"Are we there yet?" asked Meg.

"Just say if you think we've found a good spot," Ngozi called back.

They struggled on a bit further until the vegetation thinned out a little. There was a wider path and they walked together. Further ahead was a pond. Beyond that were thick brambles with vicious looking thorns.

"How about next to the pond?" suggested Emily.

"Yeah," Ngozi replied, "The soil will be softer there. Easier to dig."

As they approached the pond, the stench of the stagnant water urgently arrived in their nostrils. The piercing sun sliced through the trees above and had dried out the edges of the pond completely. Clouds of biting insects flung themselves in crazy circular motions here and there. The trees rustled above the girls as birds fled in terror at their approach.

Emily pointed to a dark patch of mud close to them. It had a thin layer of dead leaves on top.

"There?"

Meg went over and poked the ground with her foot.

"Feels squishy," she said, "Looks good to me."

Ngozi dumped the backpack on the floor.

"Be careful," Emily said.

"We're about to bury it," Meg snorted, "I really wouldn't worry if it breaks."

"Just be careful with it."

Ngozi scooped the leaves away then opened the backpack. Emily took the doll out and laid it gently on the concrete path. It looked to her like a small child had been left in a hit and run.

"Who wants what?" Ngozi said lifting the garden tools.

"I want the scratchy thing," Meg said taking the three-pronged, clawed tool.

Emily took one trowel and Ngozi took the other.

"Let's dig," Emily said and plunged the trowel into the soft soil.

Meg scratched at the surface and Ngozi twisted and turned the trowel making the soft earth even softer for Emily to dig. They had made a large hole in very little time. They put the tools down next to newly deposited pile of dirt.

"Shall I put her in?" asked Ngozi.

"No, I'll do it," Emily replied.

She wondered why Ngozi called the doll 'her' when they had all been saying 'it' up until now. She didn't like it being called her. It made what they were doing seem even stranger, wrong even. Like they were getting rid of a body. She looked around to make sure no one was coming, making that same feeling even weirder.

"I'll keep a look out in case someone comes," said Meg, standing.

Emily realised that Meg must have been thinking and feeling the same thing. She lifted the doll with two hands. The hair hung down toward the freshly dug grave. Emily placed the doll down and flicked the hair away from the lifeless face.

The eyes looked a brilliant blue in the bright sunshine. They stared directly at Emily. The red smile on tiny lips seemed to have faded a little though. She looked sad and lost. She would be alone in the earth. In her grave.

Emily shook her head a little. Perhaps she was trying to shake away the thoughts that tumbled in her head around and around, like a stuffed animal being cleaned in a washing machine. Or a doll.

"This is so weird," Emily said at last.

"Yeah, so let's get it done," Ngozi replied reaching down with her trowel.

"No," Emily said snatching hers up, "It has to be me. He was my cousin and it belonged to him."

"Should we say something?" asked Meg biting her lip.

Emily paused. Perhaps they should. Perhaps this was all part of her grieving process. Perhaps there was ceremony in it.

"Nah," Ngozi interrupted Emily's thought processing, "Get it in the ground."

Meg shrugged and looked in each direction of the path. Emily nodded and began to heave lumps of soil onto the doll.

She didn't start with the face. That would be wrong. So, she started at the feet and made her way up. First, its tiny white toes disappeared under the jet-black wet soil. Then the dress with frills was covered. Finally, her head. Her porcelain head with unblinking eyes. Her long hair with a slight wave in it.

No, not *her,* it. It was a thing. Not a *her*. Why was she thinking like this?

Then, it was done.

Emily slowly stood up.

She dropped the trowel and it landed with a soft thud onto the soil. She looked at her friends who were looking at her.

"Done," Ngozi said, "Now let's put all of this behind us. Shall we go to Starbucks?"

"Yeah," said Meg, "I want some iced tea. It's hot now."

"Let's drop off the tools at mine first," Emily said, "I need to wash my hands. A lot. In bleach."

The others laughed. Ngozi then stuffed the tools into her backpack and they all set off.

"You fancy coming to meet Liam and that lot tonight?" Ngozi asked Meg.

"Yeah!" she said a little too enthusiastically, "Will Khalid be there?"

"Yeah and Jason," Ngozi said leaning over to look at Emily.

"I don't like Jason," said Emily indignantly.

"Well he likes you," Ngozi laughed, "Liam told me."

Emily shrugged,

"I'm at dance anyway."

"Sack it off!" Meg said nudging her.

"I said that," added Ngozi.

"Nah, I want to go. I have a competition coming up."

The three of them argued about this all the way to Emily's house. But, at last, her friends gave up trying to persuade her. They had done this so many times before but knew that Emily was committed to her dance classes. She had her medals and trophies on display. She was proud of what she could do. It was part of who she was.

At her home, the garden tools were returned and hands were washed. Then the house was locked and the three headed off to the shopping centre up the road. They saw other groups from school making the same journey but didn't acknowledge them. Even when some girls at the park called and waved to them, they ignored them. They weren't deliberately being rude, they were just too involved in their own conversations.

But despite the constant chat, Emily's thoughts kept returned to the doll in the ground.

Chapter Eleven

That evening, after dance, Emily was collected by Paul. He chatted to her about stuff but she didn't reply much. At last, he put some music on he thought she might like.

She was often tired after dance but that was not why she was unresponsive. Her thoughts were with the doll beneath the earth.

Some part of her was dreading the night. Some part of her half expected the doll to be back on her drive pointing an accusatory finger up at her.

Of course, she knew this to be ridiculous. Of course, it was laughable to even conceive of such a thing. Yet, the thought was there. Like an awkward stain on her mind, it just wouldn't go.

Dance had been a distraction and a welcome one. But now images of the doll having soil heaped upon its tiny body and face were all Emily could see. The little girl below the ground.

But it wasn't a little girl. It was a porcelain thing with something like horse hair made in a factory. It was an inanimate object and nothing more. She hadn't seen it move. It hadn't written something on the mirror. She was being ridiculous and that was that.

What could it do to her anyway? It was like people who were scared of spiders. They were tiny, in this country anyway, they weren't poisonous, so what could they do? Yet people had irrational, instinctive fears of them.

Was that what this was? An *instinctive* fear? She pondered this as the car rolled up onto the drive. Why was she afraid of the doll?

In reality if it walked up to her she could kick it flying through the air. Surely a little porcelain thing couldn't hold any strength. She laughed out loud.

"What's funny?" asked Paul.

She ignored the question as they went into the house.

"Hi Mum," she called upon stepping inside.

Yes, it was absurd to be afraid of a silly little thing.

"Can I have a hot chocolate?" she called.

"I'll make it," Paul said brushing past her.

He busied himself with Nesquik and milk. He microwaved it for one minute and ten seconds. He always reckoned that was the best temperature but she really wasn't bothered.

"Thanks, Paul," she smiled at him and gave him a brief hug.

Emily then took the mug up to her Mum's room. Catherine was already in bed reading a magazine.

"Hi, love," she said smiling from behind the glossy pages.

"Hi Mum," said Emily sitting at the end of the bed.

"How was today?" her Mum asked, "You doing ok?"

She nodded.

"You?"

Her Mum shrugged.

"You know," was all she replied.

"Why don't you take time off work?"

"Work helps."

Emily nodded.

"Unless you need me to?" Catherine then said quickly, "Do you? Do you want me to be at home with you?"

"No, I'm fine," Emily spoke deliberately slowly, emphasising each word, "Really."

"OK," smiled her Mum.

They chatted for a little while. Then Paul came up and brushed his teeth. Emily did the same then told them she was going to sleep. But sleep was not near. She just knew it.

She laid in her bed with her headphones and iPad. She watched the first few episodes of Stranger Things Season One. The house was silent and still. But then came that rumbling again. Another storm? Again? But this time it seemed far away and less intense.

To her surprise she started nodding off so turned out the light and watched a bit more. Then she fell fast asleep with the iPad still churning out episode after episode. Her headphones had fallen to the side of her pillow. Season One ran into Season Two. She had seen it a few times before but now the TV show was playing to an absent audience. The storm quietly raged somewhere in the distance. Emily slept on.

Her eyes snapped open. She sat up in her bed. The duvet was by her feet and no longer up to her chin. She had felt it being yanked from the bed. An instant chill covered now instead of the warmth of the duvet. Goosebumps pricked her flesh everywhere. She wildly looked around the room. Moving in slow motion; cautiously, nervously, she grabbed the duvet from the floor. She pulled it back up to herself and peered at the bottom of the bed.

Her head turned to look at the clock. Three thirty-three AM.

She gulped. Of course, it was.

She turned on the light and scanned her room. She knelt and peered down at the bottom of the bed. Nothing.

The duvet hadn't been pulled away. It was her imagination. It was three thirty-three because her body was used to waking up that time. She remembered a conversation she had had with Paul about this very subject. He always woke at six AM even at weekends. He didn't even really need his alarm but always set it as his body clock had trained itself to wake at this time for work.

She laid back down with a long sigh. She tucked the duvet around her body and laid her head on her pillow. Her hands were stuck under her chin holding on to the duvet. Then she reached out to turn off the light.

As soon as she did the duvet was pulled with incredible force from her hands and body. She let out a startled shriek and sat up. She was up against the bed head with her arms wrapped around her knees.

Her eyes darted this way and that. It had definitely happened that time. There was no denying it.

She wanted to run from the room but she couldn't. She wanted to cry out but she found no voice. Her throat was dry and her breathing rasped.

There was no movement in her room. It was utterly still. Only her eyes moved. They flicked from side to side, up and down. Waiting for what was next. But there was nothing.

Eventually, after seconds had ticked by as slow as hours. She put her hands down on the bed. Then back to her knees. Then the bed.

When there was still nothing she leaned forward a little to look at the duvet. It sat innocently partly on the floor and partly on the bed. She grabbed it and slowly pulled it, slowly at first, then a little faster. But then she stopped. There was resistance.

Something was pulling back.

She tugged with a swift movement but something was holding on. *Holding* on. With strength.

She gave a quick yank and the grip from the other end was released. She fell backward with a light thud against the head board.

Suddenly the duvet was flung over the top of her. She screamed out and flapped her arms at it. She began to hysterically cry out as she flung the duvet off the bed.

Then her light was on. Then her Mum was in her room. So was Paul. She screamed and pointed to the base of the bed.

She made incomprehensible noises.

Paul lifted up the duvet and held it in his arms with a look of confusion.

"What was it?" he asked, "What's wrong Emily?"

Her Mum was on the bed with her arms around the sobbing girl. Paul was walking around the bed, torch in hand.

"There's nothing," he said, "It's all fine."

Emily wiped her tears and sat up.

"I'm sorry," she said at last, "It must have been a bad dream."

But she didn't believe her words. She had *felt* the duvet being pulled from her hands.

"What was it?" asked her Mum.

"I don't know really," Emily whispered, looking away, "The duvet was sort of being pulled from me."

"Your Mum gets that a lot," smiled Paul.

Catherine smiled back.

"Yeah, a lot."

She stroked Emily's hair.

"Do you want to come in with me?'

Emily shook her head. She wasn't seven. She was being ridiculous. Again. It probably was a bad dream. She probably had imagined it.

"I'm ok," she said, wiping her eyes and nose, "Really. Go back to bed. I'm going to get some sleep."

"You sure?" asked Paul, "You want a hot chocolate or hot milk or anything?"

"I'll stay here until you go to sleep," her Mum said.

Emily groaned. She hated all this fuss.

"No, I'm fine. Just get some sleep. Please."

The two reluctantly left after more protests. Emily was alone. She nervously looked around her room. Her duvet was back on the bed and she was under it. Her Mum had smoothed it down and it was like a still ocean. A calm before a storm? She looked at her clock. Three fifty-two AM. She was pretty certain that there were no crazy stories about events happening to people at *that* time.

But had she really had a bad dream? It was possible she supposed. But the feeling of the duvet being yanked away was so real.

She slid from the bed and looked around her room. She checked under the bed. Then went through every drawer. Looked behind the curtains at the windowsill. The windows were shut. She then checked the wardrobe. She looked in the bags on her floor. There was nothing.

Nothing was untoward.

It had been her imagination and nothing more.

She slid back under the covers and let out a long sigh. Her head rested on the pillow. She stayed like this for a while with the light on. Her eyes were heavy. Her breathing grew long and deep. It had a rich rhythm to it. Her blinking became slow and sometimes her eyes remained shut for a few seconds.

Emily reached out to turn off the light. She might get a few hours' sleep and feel better in the morning.

Suddenly her whole head was pulled backward by her hair. She felt fingers wrapped tightly and they were pulling. Hard.

She let out a stifled scream and reached behind her. Her hair was too long for her to find what was pulling her hair. But the fingers were small. The strength immense.

She stopped leaning forward and slammed her head backward then the grip was released.

She whirled around to find the doll but there was nothing there.

Standing by the side of the bed, she made fists with her fingers and scanned the room madly.

More time passed. She crept around the bed toward the side the doll had been on. There was nothing there.

Why was she so convinced it was the doll? Perhaps she had just caught her hair under her iPad or something. Perhaps it had got stuck between the mattress and bed. Perhaps . . .

She was running out of things it could have been.

She moved around her room looking under clothes lying on the floor. She searched again in drawers and the wardrobe.

This was crazy. Was she crazy? Was she actually losing her mind? The loss of her cousin was probably having more an effect on her than she thought. Her aunt and uncle had gone too. This was her family. People grieved in a variety of ways. Stress affected people in numerous and strange ways. She remembered Paul telling her that too.

She sat at her dressing table and knew that sleep would not come now. She didn't want to get into that bed. She didn't want to be in this room.

Tapping her knees, she looked around. This was her haven. Her safe place. A place of solace and solitude but now it felt different. She hated it.

It was all because of that stupid doll. Why had Kyle brought it back? Why did he have to die?

She hated him too. She hated everything and everyone at that moment. Including herself. And it was while she was busy hating that she felt it.

A sharp and deep scratching against the back of her legs. She winced and let out a small, high pitched, 'ow'. Emily looked down and saw one of her calves was bleeding.

"Ow," she said louder this time, looking at the small wound.

She took a tissue from her dressing table and wiped at the blood. Four scratches about five centimetres each ran down her skin. They looked like the scratches a small child could make. Or a doll.

Chapter Twelve

Emily had spent the rest of the night on the sofa downstairs, thinking and looking at her phone. She tried to make sense of it all but kept coming up empty handed.

Had the duvet been pulled? Probably not. Maybe not. Had her hair been pulled? Perhaps. Or not. Had she been scratched by something? Definitely. She had cleaned the wound with a disinfectant wipe she found in the medicine box in a kitchen cupboard and added a plaster.

It was there. There was no denying it. What wasn't clear was what had made the wound. There was nothing under her dressing table. Or under the stool she had been sat on.

Early morning light crept across the room. She heard Paul's alarm clocking going off. He usually switched it off before it rang so as not to disturb her Mum but he must have been tired. He would be downstairs any minute to make both himself and her Mum tea. She felt a stab of guilt. It was her fault he was tired. She got up and put the kettle on. She might as well make herself useful and keep busy. That was what her Mum always said helped. That was why her Mum was going to work every day when her sister had just died.

Paul jumped when he saw her then he laughed.

"Are you ok?"

He gave her a small hug then started making her a hot chocolate.

"Yeah, sorry about last night. Think I had another bad dream or something."

"It's bound to happen."

The microwave beeped several times and Paul handed her a steaming mug.

"Swap you," he said.

She handed him the two teas after setting her drink on the side. He collected them and went upstairs.

"Is it ok if Ngozi and Meg stay over tonight?"

"Yeah, course," he called back.

She had to do something tonight. She could have just stayed at one of their houses. She could hide. But it just wasn't who she was.

A long sigh escaped her chest. Was this all in her head? She looked down at her leg. No. It wasn't. Yet to be certain, her friends could stay over. They would either experience something or they wouldn't. Either way it would help Emily.

She flopped down onto the sofa and scooped up her phone. She messaged Ngozi and Meg in a small group chat on Instagram that was constantly monitored.

'stay at mine tonight?'

'yeah'

'yez. anything happen last night'

'loads'

'REALLY? what?'

'come over ill tell u'

'be there soon'

'me 2'

She got up and walked cautiously to her room. But it had lost its sinister feeling slightly from earlier. Somehow the fear was driven away by the daytime. She shook her head. Holding the door handle, she hesitated though. Do creepy things only happen at night?

She let going of the handle. Then she turned and decided to brush her teeth in the bathroom. She looked at herself in the mirror. Dark circles were under her eyes and her hair was a mess. She had a pale complexion at the best of times but she looked like a ghost. Nothing makeup wouldn't fix though, she thought.

Her eyes moved away from the glass and looked into the sink instead. When her electric toothbrush told her she was done, she wiped the sink and put the toothbrush in the cabinet above the sink.

Then she went back to her room and paused once more. She pushed it open with her foot and took a tentative step forward. She peered around the door and into the room. It looked just as it had done last night. She squatted to look under the dressing table.

Nothing.

She heard herself sigh again then sat and brushed her hair. It was so thick and very long. She was teased about it a lot but she actually liked it. It had seemed to have become socially acceptable to make fun of people with ginger hair. But how was it any different to making racist comments? Why should anyone be treated any differently just because of the colour of their skin or eyes or hair? It made no sense to Emily as to why people didn't think the same as her.

Then there was a flash of movement in the mirror. Something had darted past behind her. She turned but there was nothing there. It was probably just a bird flying past her window.

She was so jumpy. But no sleep and her creepy experiences were bound to have an effect on her. Plus, Kyle.

She would maybe put a picture of him up in her room. But not yet.

Her straighteners were plugged in and she waited for the blinking red light. There was another long sigh. But then something moved past her in the mirror again.

Whirling around, she stood up this time.

She took a step toward the window and looked all around her room. Her heart thudded and pounded in her chest. She thought she could hear footsteps behind her and spun around to face the other way.

"Emily," her mother called and knocked on her door.

Then Catherine came in. Emily raced to her and gave her a hug.

"You look awful!" her Mum exclaimed, "I'm taking the day off."

Emily composed herself. It took concentration and effort but she did it and even managed a smile.

"No, no. Its ok. I'm just tired. Sorry about last night. Ngozi and Meg are coming around in a bit."

"Shall I stay until they're here?"

"No, I'll come into your room and finish getting ready in there though."

She scooped up a pot of brushes and makeup bag and led her Mum to her room.

"Right, bye you two," Paul said brushing past them both on the landing, "Text if you need anything."

Emily stood by the bed and faced a mirror on the wall.

"How's things at work anyway?"

Catherine looked surprised. Emily never asked her anything about her work. But she wanted to talk about something, *anything*, so as not to think about what was going on around her.

Her Mum chatted away about this and that. She worked for the council in a learning resources department. Basically, she picked interesting artefacts, objects, books and posters for primary schools linked to their topics. But there had been major budget cuts meaning that staff had been sacked and there wasn't much money to buy new resources. Delivery drivers, admin staff, trainers, all had been reduced dramatically. School budgets were tight too and so less schools were subscribing to the service.

Emily knew as much as that anyway but what her Mum was now chatting about was the politics of the place and the clash of personalities.

She applied her foundation and mascara as she gave the occasional 'yeah', 'really' or 'no way'.

When she was finished, Emily sat on the bed listened for a bit longer. Suddenly her Mum gave a small gasp,

"Look at the time! I'd really better go. Are you sure you're ok?"

"Yeah, go, go," she said but didn't mean it.

Catherine kissed Emily's cheek and hurried down the stairs. Then the front door was closed and she was off.

Emily was alone in the house. She looked at the clock in the room. Seven forty-five. There was no way Ngozi and Meg would be round soon. She was pretty amazed that they had replied to her message before seven AM. They had said an hour but she knew it wasn't going to happen. Especially not Meg.

She was still sat on the bed. Unsure of what to do. Maybe watch TV downstairs? Go for a walk?

Her phone was in her pyjama pocket. She took it out and typed,

'can I cum to 1 of urs now?'

'mine is fine'

She smiled. It was Ngozi.

'on my way'

'see u soon'

'ill be there soon too'

The smile remained as she stood up. She needed to dress quickly and get out of there now.

She went to her room swiftly but slowed down when she opened the door. She peered into the bedroom. Her eyes flicked this way and that then she went inside. She took off her pyjamas after she had found some Calvin Klein pants from the drawer. She slid these on and then she put on short Nike socks. She picked up her New Look skinny jeans from the floor. She slipped these on too and went into her drawer to find a white eleven degrees T shirt. Her phone was put into her back pocket and she opened her wardrobe to find a hoodie.

As she slid the door open a bag fell from a shelf at the top. The contents fell out and banged off her head. She let out a startled shriek and stepped backward instinctively putting her hands onto her head. She rubbed it briefly and looked at what had fallen.

It was Kyle's DVDs and Pop Vinyls that had fallen. They lay scattered on the floor. The Tesco bag that they had been in was on its side still in the wardrobe. Its gaping empty mouth leered at her. She turned and left the room without picking them up. Still rubbing her head, she hurried down the stairs.

Then she stopped. Her keys were upstairs. She considered leaving the house without locking it.

She groaned and quietly rushed up the stairs. She didn't even look around her room but simply swiped the keys from her dressing table and sprinted back down the stairs.

She locked up and didn't exactly run but certainly walked at a quick pace to Ngozi's.

"You're early!" Reggie exclaimed as he was getting into his car.

She smiled and waved to him.

"Can I just go in?"

"Of course! You don't need to ask!"

He started the engine and reversed off the drive, waving to her the whole time.

She walked into the house and said hello to Ngozi's Mum before going upstairs to her room.

"Hey," Ngozi said as she walked in.

Ngozi was in her dressing gown sitting on the bed with her phone in her hand.

"Hey," she said back.

She then sat up as Emily sat on the bed.

"Well, tell me everything."

Her smile was wide and her eyes had a sparkle to them. Emily slumped backwards and groaned loudly.

"I'm losing my mind," she said with her eyes closed and a pained expression upon her face.

"Tell me," Ngozi said encouragingly.

Still laid upon the bed with eyes closed Emily began,

"So, last night I felt the duvet being pulled out of my hand. I put it back and it happened again.

"Then I felt my hair being pulled. I gave up trying to sleep and sat on my stool. Then something scratched my leg."

"No way."

"Look!"

She sat up and held her leg out. She pulled up the jean leg to show the large plaster.

"So, I gave up trying to sleep and went downstairs. But then when I'm getting ready this morning something kept moving behind me. Then, when I open my wardrobe the bag with Kyle's things in tipped over, *by itself*, and landed on my head."

At this Ngozi started laughing. Emily looked at her incredulously but then found herself laughing too.

She then made a frustrated sound and shook her head.

"I mean it could just be my imagination, couldn't it? That's why I want you to stay at mine tonight. To see if I'm going mad or not.

"I mean the duvet and my hair being pulled could have been my imagination I guess. Maybe. The thing moving this morning could have been nothing. Kyle's bag might just have been me opening the wardrobe door.

"But this . . ."

She slowly peeled the plaster backwards and showed Ngozi the four, finger shaped scratches on her leg. It was then that Ngozi stopped smiling. A frown fell upon her face. She looked on wide eyed and frightened.

Chapter Thirteen

Meg arrived about half an hour later. Her long blonde hair was straightened to perfection. She wore mascara and lipstick. Her fake tan wasn't too fake. She wore skinny, ripped black jeans and a Ted Baker crop top.

"What have I missed?" she asked.

Emily used pretty much exactly the same words she had with Ngozi.

"Show her the scratch though," Ngozi interrupted.

Emily lifted up the plaster. Meg shrugged.

"I've scratched myself like that in my sleep before," she said.

Emily made a 'hmm' noise and shrugged too.

"Your fingers are bigger than that," Ngozi said, "That scratch is doll sized!"

"Nah," Meg shrugged again, "Its nothing."

Emily pondered this for a moment or two. Her friend was probably right, which was why she wanted them around. She was being ridiculous on her own. Her Mum had her own issues right now. So, it was over to these two.

Ngozi said,

"Maybe."

Then went off for a shower and to brush her teeth.

Emily and Meg sat and looked at their phones showing each

other posts and sharing opinions about what people had put. This was what Emily needed, normality of some sort.

"You see the video of that giant snake being fed by that little girl?" Meg asked.

"No," Emily replied, "Show me."

Meg nodded at Emily's phone.

Emily messaged,

'hmu'

'DM me then I can snd it'

'here'

'here'

Emily started laughing.

"She strokes its head and everything!"

Ngozi was back in the room. She put on Adidas leggings with a Vans T shirt. She spent time straightening her hair listening to Emily and Meg.

"What you fancy doing later?"

"We could get the bus somewhere?" Emily suggested.

"We could just go straight to yours, you mean," Meg snorted, "Let's get this spooky stuff out of the way."

"I feel like we're Scooby Doo-ing this a bit much though," Ngozi said.

"No way," Meg laughed, "More like Buffy the Vampire Slayer."

"Joss Whedon is bringing that back, you know," Emily added.

"Geek," said Ngozi throwing a pillow at her friend.

The three of them chatted for a while then set off to Emily's house. She would have preferred to have spent the day shopping or hanging out somewhere then dealing with her house tonight. But Meg had been insistent and she was probably right. The bag had fallen that very morning. The weird things that had been happening were not just restricted to night time.

Plus, with her Mum and Paul being at work, it would be easier to deal with this now.

They walked from Ngozi's house via a shop to buy iced tea and smoothies for breakfast.

Emily approached her house with caution. But the two friends either side of her helped enormously. She breathed in deeply and put the keys in the lock. The three of them stood in the hallway and looked up the stairs. Shafts of light beamed down from the window at the top of the stairs. Trees outside separated the sun into individual parts making shadow patterns on the stairs.

Emily led, and they ascended slowly toward her room.

She kept her eyes fixed on her bedroom door as they approached. She couldn't help it. Taking the door handle in her hand, she pushed the door slowly open. She stepped inside and looked around. The contents of Kyle's bag were still upon the floor. DVDs and Pop Vinyls were scattered across the carpet. She looked up at the gaping mouth of the bag lolling slightly from the wardrobe.

Meg brushed past her and pulled the bag down to the floor. She began stuffing the contents back inside.

"See?" she said, "There's nothing behind. This is all just the stress of it all. Kyle's dearth. Burying that doll thing. It's all just making you think things that aren't there. The bag fell. End of. There's no drama here. No possessed doll running around scratching you. It's just normal things that are happening."

Emily was nodding. Ngozi said nothing.

Meg shoved the bag back onto the shelf and slid the wardrobe door closed.

"Right," she said, "Now what was it?"

She began searching the room; looking behind curtains, into drawers and under the bed.

"What was what?" Emily asked.

"What other things do we need to check out? The bag and what else?"

"Erm," Emily bit her lip in thought, "Well, nowhere really."

"Right, done though."

Meg flopped onto the bed.

"Starbucks?" she asked.

Emily laughed.

"Yeah, let's get out here," she said, "It's this place that's stressing me out."

She left first then the other followed. They walked up to the local shopping centre and met others from school there. They looked in a few shops, sat in Starbucks for a while then went to the park. After a McDonalds lunch they went back to the park, back to the shops and back to Starbucks. By late afternoon, they had no money and were hungry for some real food.

"My Mum will make us something," Emily said, "She should be back soon."

"I need to go to mine to get some stuff to stay over at yours," Meg said.

"Yeah, I need to do that too," Ngozi added.

"OK, meet you at mine in ten?" Emily asked.

"You gonna be ok on your own?" asked Ngozi.

She nodded in reply. Then the three parted and Emily entered the house alone. She stood in the hallway looking up at the stairs. A shiver of fear trickled down her spine. Perhaps she would wait here for them. It was only ten minutes.

But Meg was right. Nothing had happened really. She had a scratch on her leg. So what? She shook her head and went into the kitchen. She poured a glass of water and gulped it down.

"Emily."

She whirled around but there was no one there.

It wasn't Meg or Ngozi or her Mum. The voice whispered her name. Not a voice she recognised. It was in her ear loud and close.

"Who's there?" she heard herself asking.

She felt foolish and alone.

Taking a few steps across the kitchen, away from the sink, she heard it again.

"Emily."

The glass fell from her hand and shattered upon the wooden floor. The voice had been right in her ear.

She stood. Frozen. The familiar feel of locked limbs returned. Her eyes were everywhere though.

"EMILY!"

The voice screamed in her ear and she felt strong arms push her from behind. She fell onto the smashed glass with a thud and a crunch. She cried out as broken glass pierced her forearms and knees. She leapt up and ran from the room, she slipped on some glass and nearly fell again. She arrived at the front door as Meg was entering.

She pushed past her friend and slammed herself into the porch door.

"What's wrong?"

Meg grabbed her as she asked this.

Emily pointed to the kitchen. She hysterically told her what had just happened using disjointed phrases. Meg held on to her firmly with both hands.

"You dropped a glass and gave yourself a shock," she said with equal firmness to her grip, "You're fine, Emily. Really, you are fine."

Emily looked at her friend. She stared right into her eyes and slowed her breathing down back to normal.

"Yeah," she said, "Yes, I am."

Ngozi walked through the door.

"What happened?" she asked.

The three of them went into the kitchen and Emily explained pointing to the glass.

"Oh my God," Ngozi said, "You actually heard your name?"

Emily nodded.

"Or you thought you did," Meg said carefully stepping over the shattered glass.

"Why would she drop a glass if she didn't hear it?" Ngozi asked, "Plus the third time it was *shouted* in her ear. It's pretty hard to mistake that for something else. I'm pretty sure if I heard my name being shouted in my ear then I would know it was happening."

"Well, yeah, but maybe I . . . didn't. Maybe I did just imagine it. The wind or something."

Ngozi sighed and stepped over the glass too. She took a dustpan and brush from the cupboard beneath the sink and began sweeping. Meg was picking up larger shards of glass and wrapping them in the local newspaper that sat on the worktop.

Soon the mess was gone and Emily still stood in the same place. Blood trickled down her jeans and onto the floor. Her elbows were cut too but not bleeding.

She saw her friends looking at her legs and looked down. She groaned and went into the kitchen cupboard for wipes and plasters. She cleaned herself up as Ngozi wiped the blood from the floor with multi surface wipes.

"Does it hurt?" asked Meg.

Emily shook her head. They went up to her room and she changed from jeans to leggings.

"Let's watch a film or something," Ngozi suggested.

Just then, Emily's Mum walked through the door downstairs. They all went down to see her.

"Hi girls," she said as she walked into the kitchen.

"Hi," Meg said.

"Hi Catherine," said Ngozi.

"Hi Mum. Can we have some food?"

Her Mum sighed. She looked at Emily with eyes that said 'I've just walked through the door' but didn't actually say the words.

"I've got some cheese filled pasta. Any good?"

All three nodded then went off up the stairs back to Emily's room. They laid on the bed and Emily grabbed her iPad.

"What shall we watch?"

"That screens too small," Meg said, "Let's watch something downstairs."

"OK, like what?"

"The first Conjuring?" Meg suggested.

"Yeah with Annabelle in it?" laughed Ngozi without humour, "Maybe not."

Meg laughed too,

"Oh yeah. Well we could just search Netflix and see what's on."

They agreed and went downstairs. They closed the living room door and ended up watching a film where fairies, elves and orcs were real and lived in Los Angeles.

Catherine walked in holding two plates of food.

"You're all looking at your phones when there's a film on the TV," she said shaking her head.

She handed the plates to Ngozi and Meg.

"Yours is coming," she said to Emily.

"Thanks, Mum."

Her friends thanked Catherine too.

When Emily was given her food, the door was closed again. Paul opened it a few moments later, waved hello then closed it again.

The film finished and they watched a few episodes of the first season of Thirteen Reasons Why.

They eventually went up to Emily's room and started getting ready for bed. They brushed their teeth then put on pyjamas and slides on their feet. Paul arrived with an already inflated blow up bed.

"Who gets it this time?" he asked after knocking at the door.

He slid the bed next to Emily's double bed then went off to get a sheet, duvet and pillow.

"Who's turn is it?" asked Emily.

"Yours," Ngozi said pointing to Meg.

"No, because I had to sleep on one at yours last time."

"Yeah but I slept on it the last time we stayed *here*. That's the way it works."

"She's right," Emily said smiling, "You came up with that rule."

Meg started laughing,

"I know. I just thought I'd try."

Paul was back and put the sheet onto the bed. Then he left the pillow and duvet in a small pile on top.

"Hot chocolate?" he asked.

They all answered 'yes' and he went off again.

Emily looked out of the window. Her eyes wandered down the street toward the nature reserve. She blinked them closed and shut the curtains firmly.

Ngozi and Meg were in bed looking at their phones. Emily was so glad that they were there. She felt safe. For the first time since Kyle's death, she felt as if her room was not a sinister place. Climbing into her bed she felt exhausted. She knew that she would sleep safely and soundly in her bed.

Chapter Fourteen

THE THREE GIRLS WERE sound asleep.

The white alarm clock with the red numbers glowed softly in the dark. The time was three thirty-two. A bed side lamp hung over the clock. The fat bulb began to fizz and flicker. Emily groaned and turned over in her sleep toward her bedside table. The light hummed and buzzed then was still.

She awoke and opened her eyes. Through thin slits she looked at the clock. Three thirty-three AM.

She made another groaning sound and sat up. The duvet rustled as she shoved her back against the head board. Ngozi snored very softly beside her. Meg was face down on her pillow below on top of the inflated, now slightly deflated, blow up bed.

All was quiet and still. Except for her. She was awake. At the same time. Again.

But nothing was happening. There was no paranormal activity. There was no conjuring of dolls. There was just her and her friends in her room having a sleepover.

Perhaps this had all just been in her head.

Then the bedside lamp flickered again and she heard a creaking of a floorboard. She knew the floorboards of the stairs well. She knew where to step on which stair. From the top to the bottom it went something like left, left, middle, left, right, middle –. Her thought process was interrupted by another creak. It was a low-pitched squeaking sound.

Houses often made sounds like this. It was totally normal.

Then another.

Someone was coming up the stairs.

The sounds were very soft and quiet. It wasn't her Mum and Paul. She knew their footsteps. She knew individually how they walked. She hadn't heard them going down the stairs either. This was someone, a very light someone, ascending the stairs right this second.

She shook Ngozi gently. The girl groaned and opened her eyes.

"What time is it?" she asked sleepily.

Not answering Emily leaned over the other side of the bed.

"Meg," she hissed.

Meg made a sort of snuffling sound but didn't move. There was another creak from the stairs.

"*Meg*," she said more insistently now and louder too.

Meg sat straight up.

"What's happening?"

Ngozi was sat up now too. Emily flicked on the bedside table lamp. The room took some time to light up properly as the energy saving bulb was still as tired as the girls. Tired but now fully awake.

"Did you hear that?" Emily asked in an urgent whisper.

"What?" Meg hissed back.

There were two more creaks on the stairs outside.

"That!" Emily said pointing toward the door.

"Yeah, I heard it," Ngozi said grabbing Emily's arm.

More creaking sounds could be heard. Slightly louder now. Closer.

Meg got up. She stretched her arms and back then took two steps toward the door.

"What are you doing?" Emily whispered loudly.

Meg turned around with a slightly forced nonchalant expression upon her face.

"Proving to you that its nothing."

She took the door handle in her hand then hesitated slightly as another creak was heard. She turned it but the door didn't open. She was more forceful but still the door didn't budge. She made a small grunting sound with the effort but it was like someone was holding the door from the other side. She used both hands and still could not open the door.

Emily and Ngozi were now standing behind her.

"What's happening?" asked Ngozi.

Emily remembered when she couldn't open the door from the other side of it. She grabbed Meg's hands to help her but still the door wouldn't budge.

Then there were three hard knocks on the door and it flung open. The two girls fell backwards making Ngozi trip over the blow-up bed and land with a soft thud on top of it.

The door was wide open. Gaping and black.

Emily helped Ngozi up with one arm and flicked on her bedroom light with the other. The light from the ceiling was bright and lit up the landing slightly. The three girls peered onto the landing.

Then, cautiously, they stepped onto it and flicked the light switch on. They all saw it at the same time. Their eyes were drawn immediately to what was not right. Upon the carpet. Leading down the stairs. No. *Up* the stairs were small brown smudges of dirt. They were in pairs and followed a straight pattern. Footprints. Muddy footprints that led from the darkness below all the way up to Emily's room. They stopped right where the girls were standing.

"What the hell?" Meg exclaimed.

The three girls stepped backward as one. They retreated into the bedroom and closed the door. Then they looked at each other with so many questions behind their fearful eyes. Before anyone could speak there were three loud knocks upon the other side of the door.

"Put something up against it!" Meg shouted and began to look around the room for something heavy.

Ngozi picked up the stool and wedged it against the door.

"We need more things," Meg said adding first her bag then Ngozi's backpack.

Emily dragged her bedside cabinet over and pushed it in place.

There was more knocking. This seemed to freeze the girls in place. The knocking acted as a kind of pause button on a remote control. It's affects worked for only a few seconds then they were moving again.

"Hang on a minute," Meg said, "It's only a *doll*."

Emily and Ngozi looked at her. There was nothing rational in their actions. Was it only a doll? How could a doll hold a door and knock with such violent force? How could a doll move and leave footprints? None of it made any sense including their own actions and reactions. There was something sinister going on and that was that. They didn't want whatever was holding the door and knocking in this room and that was that.

Another three knocks sent them all, including Meg, into statues again and then a frenzy of activity. They piled up all kinds of things against the door.

Then there was nothing for a few moments.

The girls looked at the door. Then each other. Then around the room. Back to the door. Their wild eyes were everywhere. Their posture was that similar to cats about to make an alarmingly long leap. They were poised and ready. But for what?

The sound of a small girl laughing was coming from behind the door. A light, high pitched giggle. The sound of amusement.

Then creaking as soft footsteps treaded the stairs downward. It was leaving. *She* was leaving.

No one knew just what to do. They looked at each other again. Each girl knew that they were acting out a cliché. They were acting just like the people in the movies and TV shows that they all watched. But they couldn't help it. Fear held them tightly and controlled them like puppets. They danced and moved to its command.

There was a light tapping at the window. Three taps, just like there had been at the door. Tap, tap, tap. Light fingers on the glass.

"Don't open the curtains," Ngozi whispered.

"I have to see," Meg said slowly, "We have to know."

"No . . . we don't!"

Ngozi made an incredulous gesture with her hands.

"Are you mental?"

"It could be a bird or something," Meg hissed.

The tapping was heard again. Louder and faster.

Emily knew Meg was right. This was why they had stayed over with her. They had to know. *She* had to know. She needed proof that this wasn't in her head. Proof was now being offered.

She turned off the main light first and then the bedside light.

"Yeah," Ngozi whispered, "Let's pretend we've gone back to sleep. Then it will leave us alone as we're showing we're not bothered. That's the way to deal with this. Like in Nightmare on Elm Street. Show the thing it can't scare us."

She was talking quietly but very fast. Emily stepped toward the curtains.

"No," Ngozi said, louder now, more insistent, "You're not listening to me!"

Emily took the curtains in her hands. She turned and looked over her shoulder at Ngozi and Meg. They were standing by the bed with wide eyes.

"I have to," Emily said softly.

It was part apology and part exclamation. She flung open the curtains in one swift movement. She parted them with all the strength she could find and they raced open revealing the window. And the doll.

It was standing outside and to the left. Its forehead was leaning on the window, its hair streaked over the glass in wet clumps. It wasn't moving but the eyes seemed to be staring at them. It was blank and expressionless. The thin, red lips were curved ever so slightly into the smile of a reptile. The ruddy cheeks were covered in mud. As was the dress. It hung down in dirty tatters. The small fingers were curled into fists and the white porcelain was mud smeared.

No one moved. No one breathed. The doll was motionless too. They were all locked as one into this moment. Freeze framed in time.

The bed side lamp flickered and buzzed into life. It made the girls turn to look at it. It fizzed and glowed then became impossibly bright. They had to squint their eyes and then look away. The bulb popped with a loud noise and sent shards of glass exploding all around.

As the shards landed the girls looked back to the window. The doll was gone.

No one said anything for a while. Nor did they move.

"Holy shit," Meg said at last.

Ngozi let out a loud and long sigh. A huge exhaling breath. Emily was shaking all over. She took a step toward the window and looked left then right. She took another step and peered down at the deserted street.

"She's gone."

"Yeah, but where to?" Ngozi asked breathlessly.

"Holy shit," Meg said again.

Emily scanned the street several times. Then she slammed the curtains closed. She tripped over the blow-up bed on her way to the light switch and cut her foot on a shard of glass from the light bulb. She let out a sharp 'ow' sound.

The light was flicked on and she sat on her own bed to look at the small slither of glass poking from her bare toe. The pain was a welcome distraction from what had just happened.

She realised that she felt something like relief as to actually seeing the doll and that her friends had seen the same thing. She wasn't going mad. She *had* experienced these things.

"I need to leave," Meg said, "Now."

"What and go . . . *out there*?" Ngozi asked, "You really want to go outside into the dark with that . . . that *thing*?"

"Well it can get into here too!" Meg shrieked.

Her voice was loud and shrill.

"Quiet," Emily whispered, "You'll wake them up."

She flicked her head to the side toward her Mum's bedroom. She was holding the small piece of glass in her hand tipped in red.

Meg was visibly shaking all over. Her face was a pale mask of fright. Emily's eyes found the blood-stained shard of glass. She might be able to distract her friend with this.

"I cut my toe," Emily said and held it out to her two friends, "Is it bad?"

She dropped the glass into a bin which landed with a small tinkling sound then looked at the two frightened faces.

Ngozi came over and held Emily's foot in her hand.

"It's fine," she said in a small voice, "Just a little cut. Does it hurt?"

Emily shook her head.

"I need to go, seriously, you two. Let's get out of here!"

Meg's voice was raised and Emily shushed her.

"What?" Meg shrieked, "Don't wake them up? We need to wake them up! We need Paul to go and check that that thing has gone!"

Just then Paul knocked and came into the room. Catherine was behind.

"Is everything ok girls?" he asked.

"No," Meg said, crying, "I want to go home."

"Why?" asked Catherine, walking over to give her a hug, "What's happened?"

Chapter Fifteen

Paul drove Meg back to her home in silence. It was four AM and he had woken her mother with a call explaining that the girls had had a falling out. She raced into the house wordlessly. Paul sat outside the house for a few minutes but her Mum didn't come out.

Eventually, he started the engine back up, looked at the house for a moment or two then drove back to his home.

What had happened? These girls never fell out. They had been firm friends for the entire time Paul had been with Catherine which was now about seven years. Meg had seemed really scared. Maybe he would be told but probably not tonight. Sleepless nights seemed to be part of the deal at the moment.

But, after a horrific tragedy, things like this were bound to happen. He would just do his best like he always did. He would be there when needed and hang back until asked to do anything else.

He didn't have children of his own but felt like Emily was his. He never told her off and spoilt her far too much, he knew that. But he genuinely loved her like a daughter. So naturally he was worried. Worried about Catherine too. He was worried all of the time at the moment.

He parked the car back onto the drive as the first shafts of morning light came creeping across the sky. Looking up at the house, he saw Emily's light was still on but so where the downstairs lights too.

Locking the car, he went into the house. They were all in the kitchen drinking hot drinks. Tea for Catherine and hot chocolate for the girls he guessed.

"It's nothing, really," Emily was saying, "Meg just had a bad dream and wanted to go home."

Ngozi was nodding. It was more than that and they all knew it. But the subject was dropped and the girls went upstairs.

"What do you think really happened?" whispered Paul.

"I think they've fallen out," Catherine whispered back, "Meg hasn't been there for Emily since Kyle. Ngozi has and I'm guessing they've had it out. Probably told Meg she should have been more supportive."

Paul was nodding.

"It's been hard on everyone," she went on, "But they'll get over it. They're teenage girls. Falling out is part of any friendship group."

"It's been hard on you too," he said putting his arm around her, "You need anything?"

"A good night's sleep?"

"Maybe we should go on a holiday? Just the three of us?"

"There's too much to do with the house. You know that."

"We've both got leave we can take. There's another week before she's meant to be back at school. I know we weren't going away this year but we still can."

Catherine groaned.

"I just don't know if I want to. I think we need to keep things as normal as possible. For her."

"Just a suggestion," he said, giving her a hug, "Just give it some thought."

While they were hugging the girls were sat on the bed in Emily's room.

"I thought I was going mad," Emily sighed.

They spoke in hushed and urgent whispers to each other.

"I can't believe it," Ngozi said, "It's all real. A possessed doll."

"Possessed by what?"

"A ghost? A demon?"

"We buried it."

"I know."

"What shall we do?"

"I don't know."

"Is there anyone that can help?"

"Like who?"

"I dunno, like a priest or something?"

They both looked at the floor for a while. Each lost in their own thoughts.

"You can't stay here tonight," Ngozi suddenly said, "We'll stay at mine."

Emily nodded.

"What's all this mud all over the stairs?" Catherine called from downstairs.

"I don't know!" Emily shouted back.

"It leads to your room!" her Mum shouted from behind the closed door.

"Shall I clean it up?"

"No, I'll do it," Catherine said in tones of resignation and exhaustion.

There was some inaudible speaking from the landing.

"We should go back to where we buried it," Ngozi whispered, "Dig it back up."

Emily pondered this for a few moments then slowly nodded.

"Then do what with it?"

"Burn it."

Emily's eyes widened momentarily.

"Yeah, you're right," she said at last, "Let's wait for them to go to work and we'll get everything we need."

The sounds of sloshing water and scrubbing could be heard through the door. A cloth was squeezed and a deep sigh came next.

"I can remember exactly where it was," Emily went on, "Can you?"

Ngozi nodded.

They sat and waited in the bedroom. The minutes dragged like something jagged snagging on the smooth passage of time. But eventually, it was time for Paul and Catherine to go to work.

Emily's Mum made some protestations and fussed but she eventually left. Paul had offered to stay at home too. But at last the girls were finally alone. As soon as they'd gone, Ngozi and Emily got dressed. Ngozi tipped the contents of her backpack onto Emily's bed to be filled with digging and fire lighting equipment. The bag was eventually filled and just as they were about to set off Ngozi stopped.

"Wait," she said, "The doll was out of its, erm, *grave,* last night, right?"

Emily nodded.

"So, it's not a vampire. It's not going to get back into the ground during the day and only come out at night, is it?"

Emily chewed her lip.

"I think I just need to see if it's there," she said at last, "I don't know where else we would look."

Ngozi shrugged.

"Beats sitting around waiting for it to pop up again I guess."

"Yeah. I think I just need to *do something.* Know what I mean?"

Ngozi nodded.

"Yeah, me too."

They locked the house and set off toward the nature reserve. The sounds of chirping birds and a distant river filled their ears as they passed the first gate. The early morning air was cold and fresh. It was certainly cooler than it had been recently. The sky was white without a trace of blue. All cloud.

Insects hummed and buzzed along the path before them. The earth was soft and the nettles damp. A train rumbled in the distance.

Emily focused on these things. These normal, everyday things. She listened to a plane in the sky. Holiday makers off to sunny destinations. Like Kyle had been the last time she had seen him.

She flicked that thought away and focused her attention on not getting stung by damp nettles. Her mouth was firmly clamped shut and she became aware of her dry mouth. They neared the pond. The dark brown water was stagnant and still. Plants loomed downward toward their own reflections. There were fewer flying insects compared to last time.

The mound of earth and leaves looked untouched. How could that be? A bird zipped past them into a cluster of trees. It made Emily jump.

She looked back at the mound. The grave. Would the doll be there? She really didn't expect it to be.

Ngozi dropped the backpack. It landed with a soft thud onto the moss infested grass. Emily looked up and down the path and remembered Meg doing exactly that. She felt a mixture of anger and sympathy toward her friend.

She hugged Ngozi from the side.

"What's that for?" she asked.

"Being here," Emily replied.

Ngozi managed a small smile and bent down to unzip the bag. Two unusual looking insects flew slowly around them. As if checking out these strangers, wondering what they were doing. Had these same creatures been there the last time? Tiny witnesses to an odd crime of some sort.

The incessant chirping of the bird in the tree above became the only sound as Ngozi wordlessly handed Emily a trowel. She looked at it. Looked at it like it had been used to murder an unsuspecting victim. She held it like she had held a snake during a school visit to the botanical gardens. They had exotic animal handling that day and Emily had hated it.

She kneeled down, leaning slightly on an ivy infested tree. Why was she leaning? She could do a deep squat right to the floor without any difficulty at all yet here she was leaning against the rough bark. Moral support maybe?

Scraping the soft soil and leaves as Ngozi scratched at the earth with the fork was strange. She did it slowly, reverently even, just as she had when they buried the doll.

A different bird then started squawking over and over again. Was it warning them? Warding them away?

The two piles of soil they were making were getting larger but still no doll. No porcelain face or tangled hair. No tiny fingers and feet. No body.

They dug deeper still but they both knew that it was useless. After a while, Ngozi stopped.

She looked at Emily. Her straight dark brown hair was lifted over her darker still eyes. Her large lips made a sympathetic smile.

"It's not here," she said.

"I know."

Emily put down her trowel and looked up. A tangled knot of branches matched her mind. The air was crisp and clear but that was about the only thing that was. The leaves swayed rhythmically in the slight breeze.

"Emily."

It was the voice of a little girl. The voice she had heard before. The voice of a doll.

She whirled around to see the source of the sound. Ngozi's eyes bulged enormously. They both grabbed each other's hands.

"Emily."

It was behind them. They turned to that direction and took a step backwards as one.

The voice was foreign sounding. It was rich and exotic but here, in the woods by a pond, it seemed so out of place. It was an echoing sound that seemed not to belong in any place really.

"Emily."

It was behind them again but how could that be? It was everywhere.

"Let's go."

Ngozi's voice was shrill. She tugged Emily toward the path. She turned and looked at the back pack and tools.

"Wait, the . . ." she began but Ngozi was pulling harder now.

"Leave it!" she almost screamed.

A little girl's giggle sounded out from in front of them. They stopped instantly and wobbled uncertainly, clutching each other's hand with vice grips.

The giggle sang out again. Closer this time.

They turned and ran in the other directions but this was further in to the nature reserve. Footsteps could be heard lightly tapping on the concrete floor, following them. They turned but nothing was there. Only that giggle. High pitched and full of malice.

They ran faster but the concrete path became a wood chip one. It was soft and damp making their feet sink into the ground. It felt as if they were running over quick sand.

The sound of the footsteps had gone but the girls guessed this was only because of the change to the surface of the path. They were framed now by trees and ferns.

"Emily!"

This was in a sing song voice and appeared to be from their left.

"*Emily!*"

Louder now and to the right.

They turned and ran further. The greens were a blur as they sprinted down toward the river. Still that laugh followed them. Its shrill pitch bouncing from tree to tree.

There was a gate. Emily fumbled with the lock until Ngozi roughly pushed her to one side. She struggled for a few moments too but then it was open. The wooden slats of the gate banged against a tree with a dull thud.

They both burst through and slammed it shut. As they did, they saw her. Saw *it*.

The doll was standing on the path and staring straight at them.

Chapter Sixteen

THE TINY FIGURE WAS a statue on the path. The girls did nothing but stared and panted. How could this be? This couldn't be real. It couldn't be happening. Their brains tried to make sense of it. Tried to rationalise it somehow. But they couldn't.

This time it was Emily that snapped into action. She took Ngozi's hand and they ran down toward the river that churned and frothed. They looked back and the doll was still standing there behind the wooden slatted gate.

The brown water was fast flowing in the opposite direction to that in which they ran. Neither girl had been along this river since they were little. Neither knew how long the path was or where it led. The ground here was mostly grass on a sandy soil with moss mixed in. They could run much faster here. Eventually the gate could not be seen and they stopped.

Down here, there had been no laughing or speaking. No doll standing there staring.

Had it gone?

They held onto each other, still panting.

The path was empty in both directions. The river flowed on with white foam frothing over jutting rocks. Bull rushes waved in the wind, stabbing at the air with their sword leaves.

"Has – Has – Has it gone?" Ngozi asked in a high pitched, young girl's voice.

"I – I think so," Emily managed to reply.

They caught their breath and held on to each other for a while.

"You're right," Emily said at last, "It doesn't just come out at night."

"What do we do now?"

Emily looked around. She did not want to go back toward the woods. She did not want to go back to the pond. She tried working out where the path they were following would lead.

"I guess we just walk along here and see where it takes us to," she said, "I'm not going back there."

Ngozi nodded and picked up a thick stick from the ground. Emily now nodded and did the same. Hers felt brittle though. She would need to find a better one as they walked.

Just then, a fish jumped out of the river making a plopping sound. It also made them both jump.

Their eyes were wide and they walked with a slight crouch as if ready for something to jump out at them, which both of them were completely expecting.

There was the sound of a train in the distance. It felt very far away. As if things in the normal world were somewhere quite out of reach. In this new world, a world were dolls moved and spoke and scratched, nothing was as it seemed.

Only the river was unconcerned. Only the river was constant and unchanging. But then what dark secrets did it hold beneath its rapidly moving waters?

The path led them away from the river. They both stopped when they saw it took them back into the woods in a sort of arching, ascending path. The woodchip flooring was there too. They looked at each other. Another train rumbled far away.

"Wait," Ngozi said, "The train is that way isn't it?"

She pointed to the other side of the river. Emily nodded.

"Well the train track runs parallel to our estate. We need to be that side of the river."

"But we didn't cross the river so how can that be?"

"I mean from here it's on the other side of the river. The river doesn't run straight, does it?"

"Yeah but that doesn't make any sense," Emily protested, "Let's just follow that path."

"No, we need to cross the river."

"The path will take us back the way we came but missing out the pond and all that, I'm sure of it."

"No, the path will take us back to that doll."

"I'm sure I did this whole loop walk thing with Paul a few years ago though."

"I'm not going back into the woods."

Emily let out a startled shriek.

Ngozi looked behind her and saw the doll again. It was sitting on the path that Emily was saying they should walk up.

It looked like she was waiting for them to finish arguing and hurry up to get to her.

Ngozi ran down the slight slope and stepped onto some large rocks to cross the river. Emily raced to join her. They both stumbled and fell on the smooth stone. Their feet splashed into shallow water that slid over smaller rocks.

Then Emily felt a small hand on the back of her jeans. It tugged. Hard.

She fell forward landing onto Ngozi and they both landed to the left in the river. It was deeper here. So much deeper and fast too. The currents grabbed them and they were pulled along.

Emily grabbed at some thick pond weed but it was sleek smooth and she couldn't take hold of it. She bobbed up and down and saw Ngozi had managed to grab on to a large rock further along. She was climbing on top of it, but kept slipping down on to her knee.

Emily swam toward it, moving crazily fast. She slammed into it and heard the air escape her lungs in one massive breath.

She felt Ngozi's hands pulling her up. There were more rocks for them to stand on to get to the other side. But Emily looked all around for the tiny figure of the doll before she started moving.

The water had been utterly freezing. She was only just feeling it now as adrenaline was coursing through her body. Her soaking clothes gripped her body like they too were terrified of what would happen next.

Ngozi leapt onto the next rock and managed not to fall over by some miracle. Emily doubted she could do the same.

With a last look behind her, she then jumped and banged both knees on the rock. But she hadn't fallen into the water.

She turned to look behind again then jumped to the next rock. After two more look and jumps, they were both on the other side of the river.

They held on to each other's dripping, freezing frames and looked all around.

"Which way?" asked Emily through convulsing shakes.

Ngozi wordlessly pointed up.

They scrambled over long grasses, moist ferns and spiky plants of every sort. They gripped the solid trunks and branches of the few trees that were scattered on the slope.

At last they made it to the top and looked back down at the river and the haunted path. Nothing. She was gone. For now.

They looked in the other direction and heard the distant train once more. The woodland ahead of them looked dense but there was a path that ran parallel with the river.

"Which way?" gasped Emily.

"I have no idea," Ngozi replied, shivering.

"I think this way."

Emily pointed in the direction they had been running on the other side of the river. They jogged side by side, still dripping, still freezing. After a short time that felt like forever they came to a wooden bridge that crossed the now very wide river.

"Where the hell are we?" asked Ngozi.

Emily didn't know why she hadn't thought of it before. She took out her phone and looked at the wet and cracked screen. Ngozi did the same and groaned.

"Do we cross back over?" she asked.

"I've got no idea," Emily said, still shivering, "I think so."

They crossed the bridge and followed the path. Eventually, after half walking, half running along a grass path they came to a concrete one. This then led them toward the housing estate.

They came out of the nature reserve from a different exit from the one they knew. There was a large hill to climb then they would be back into urban safety.

"We'll get showered and changed at mine then go to yours, right?"

Ngozi didn't answer. Her skin was now paler and her lips had taken on a blue hue.

"You can shower first," Emily said.

They still scanned all around and listened intently, but the doll seemed to have stopped following them. It was leaving them alone, for some reason. For now.

Emily wasn't sure she would ever sleep again. Her heart was still pounding in her chest and it was not just down to the freezing river water.

Memories of the voice, the giggling laugh and the lifeless eyes boring into her were on a constant loop inside her mind. She guessed that Ngozi would be the same. She felt another pang of guilt that she had got her friend into this. What about Meg too? She would message her from her iPad to ask if she was alright.

Emily felt selfish for dragging these two into this. This was her horror. The doll hadn't used Ngozi's name. It was her it was after. But why? What had she done? What did the doll want from her?

'Casa'.

That single word on the mirror. It was Spanish for home. Did the doll want to be made to feel at home? All Emily had done was be repulsed by it the minute she saw it. She couldn't possibly let it live in her home now. What was she meant to do? Dress it up, give it baths and let it sleep by her side in her bed? It was completely not going to happen. No, she needed to get rid of it somehow.

Where did Kyle get it from anyway? Did it want to be back in his home? That could be worth a try. But that would mean actually touching the thing. How could she touch something that meant to harm her?

More questions rose and fell. She tried to make some sort of order with them. She tried to organise her thoughts. She imagined that if she did that then she could come up with some assort of actual realistic plan that she could begin working through. But no order could be found. No sensible, logical line of thinking could be reached. Emily supposed that logic was something that was lost to her forever. She remembered that she was now in the new world. The old one was lost and could never be regained.

They approached her house with caution. She saw one of the neighbours peer out of their window at the pair. What must they look like? Dripping wet and clinging to each other. What a sight!

Her quivering fingers found the key in her now even tighter wet jeans. She shook so badly it took both hands to wobble the key into the lock. They burst inside and kicked off wet shoes. Emily ran up the stairs and turned on the shower. Ngozi joined her and Emily found them both towels.

They showered and changed, Ngozi taking first turn, Emily next. Ngozi went to put her soaking dirty clothes, makeup, straighteners and charger into her backpack and remembered where it was. Emily loaned her friend some of her own clothes

Once dressed, Ngozi took another look at her dead iPhone then she flung it on to the bed and roared in frustration.

"Paul was going to trade in his old phones. They'll be in his office desk. I'm pretty sure there's a 6 and an SE in there."

"Won't he be mad if you take them?"

"Nah, I'll explain. I'll say we fell in the river. He won't have got much for them on eBay or at CEX anyway. He'll be ok."

Ngozi nodded and managed a smile. Emily packed a bag to go to hers. Then she sent messages via her iPad to her Mum, 'sleeping at Ngozi's. Love ya'. Then to Paul, 'taken 2 fones from yer desk will explain later. Love ya'. Finally, to Meg, 'U ok? Got loads to tell ya. Ill be at N's'.

The iPad was slid into her bag. She went and found the two phones from downstairs. Ngozi followed her. Emily looked at the 6 and the SE and without much thought handed her friend the more recent SE.

"You take that one," Ngozi said shaking her head, "I'll have the 6."

Emily insisted, then locked up and set off to her friend's house. The sky was now bright with sunshine but a foreboding sense of dread was rising inside her like a brooding storm.

Chapter Seventeen

Ngozi and Emily were laid upon the bed whispering about all that had happened that day. They'd shared a meal with Ngozi's family and pretended to be alright when that was far from the truth.

"Do you think it'll come back tonight?" asked Ngozi is hushed tones; urgent and frightened, "Do you think it'll know where we are?"

Ngozi still referred to the doll as an 'it' but Emily now found that strange. To her the doll had firmly become 'she'. It had become more than just an inanimate object. The fact that 'it' was now a 'she' didn't soften Emily's memory of that day though. If anything, 'she' had become more sinister; more real and most definitely more threatening. The 'she' Emily pictured in her mind could absolutely come back tonight and absolutely knew exactly where they were.

"No," Emily smiled at her friend, "I think we lost her in the woods. She might go to my house though. I hope she leaves my Mum and Paul alone."

Emily meant this but also just *knew* that the doll wanted her and her alone.

"We could have drowned," Ngozi said with haunted tones, "We could have died in that river."

"I know," Emily replied, "I know this is all my fault too. I'm sorry, Ngozi."

"It's not your fault. That thing was given to you in the most awful way. I just hope this is all over now."

"Has Meg replied to you?"

"Nope, she was last seen yesterday on Snapchat."

"Shall we go see her tomorrow?"

"One hundred percent."

They chatted for a while longer about the day. Sleep seemed far from a possibility and it grew later and later. Ngozi's family had gone to bed a while ago and the house was silent and still.

Emily suddenly felt the dead weight of tiredness upon her. Her legs were lead and her head felt too heavy for her neck to support. She put it on the pillow and Ngozi did the same next to her. They wordlessly turned out the light and slipped into sleep in mere minutes.

Exhaustion took Emily into a deep and dream filled sleep. She dreamt she was floating. Bobbing on water. Not the fast, churning water of the river from earlier but smooth, long and rhythmic waves. She flowed over them. She was in a thin boat that sliced the waves at speed. Cutting through the water but not at an adrenaline, racing speed, it was incredibly fast yet peaceful at the same time.

Looking up, she saw soft, white clouds tumble past. Bright blue was beyond and she found herself smiling.

Then she had stopped. The boat slid to a halt and she sat up. She had arrived at an island. All around were other islands but this one looked different. There were trees everywhere but the tree that she had come to have decorations. Christmas ones? No, the decorations were larger than baubles and didn't have shiny surfaces with ribbons and glitter. What were they?

She peered up at the trees and saw dolls. Lots and lots of dolls. Some were fully intact while others were just heads and arms and torsos. The ones with eyes all turned as one to look at her. Gaping sockets with wide eyes; staring and lifeless.

She found herself getting up from the boat and stepping ashore. The dolls then changed their blank expressions and twisted their plastic features into smiles. Their fixed faces began to laugh and giggle. Not the sinister laughing of the doll in the woods earlier though. This was the laughter of babies. High pitched and everywhere.

She walked through the trees. She knew where to go. The laughter was immense now. It filled the air and filled her ears.

Then the laughter stopped and whispering began. In was an inaudible thing but yet all around, like it could only be heard in her head. She looked up into the trees and saw the dolls no longer looked at her but looked at each other. They were whispering in hushed tones urgently to one another. The arms beckoned for each to come closer. Their heads leaned in to talk in conspiratorial tones.

She ducked under a noose like rope that hung from the trees. A line of dolls hung from it. Their tiny hands hanging down brushed the top of her head.

Then she came to a bridge. Beyond was a ramshackle hut of some sort. The bridge was lined with baby doll heads. They all turned to look at her. They had the blank expressions of toys but then their mouths twisted and contorted at exactly the same time into huge gaping smiles.

She walked between the doll's heads on the bridge. Their heads turned slightly to keep facing her as she took each step. She felt no fear though. She was being pulled magnetically toward this hut. The dolls that decorated the side of it twisted their own features into smiles too. They were welcoming her.

Emily stepped onto the decking at the entrance. A door was opened. It opened for her. She stepped inside to see every space covered in dolls. They all looked at her. They all smiled at her. Then they all looked down at the floor. Their eyes rolled in their sockets downward. She found herself doing the same.

On the ground, beneath her feet was a pillow upon a large pile of straw.

She suddenly realised that she had been holding something in her hands the whole time. She was holding a doll. The doll that had belonged to Kyle. The doll that so frightened her, yet she wasn't frightened now. Not in this dream.

She slowly and carefully placed the doll upon the pillow. It was purple and regal looking. Once she had placed the doll she felt an immense sense of relief.

She stood up straight and looked around. The dolls were now completely inanimate. The island peaceful and still.

She stood for a few moments.

Then she looked down at the familiar doll at her feet. It began to grow. Slowly at first but then at speed. It was larger than the pillow, then kept on growing until it became the same size as Emily herself. It retained its porcelain features though. It was now a human sized mannequin with lifeless eyes and a fixed gaze. That gaze was directed entirely at Emily.

They stood eye to eye, looking into each other's souls. They were locked like this for some time. The mannequin doll's blue eyes were bottomless. Black holes with unknown mysteries behind them.

Then there was darkness all around. There was no hut, no dolls, no island. There was only the mannequin doll and Emily looking upon each other. Liquid black framed the scene before Emily. There was just darkness and the oversized doll and nothing more. Then the mannequin doll's expression began to change. The features moved and shifted. Her face became utter rage. The thin lined eyebrows twisted downward, meeting each other at the point above her nose. The smooth, white porcelain skin became lined as the facial features contorted. She seemed to be breathing in and out, growing in anger second by second with nostrils flaring. The red lined mouth shrank inward and then outward revealing row after row of tiny triangular and sharp teeth. Like shark's teeth. There was the suggestion of a reptilian tongue behind.

Then the mannequin doll then leaned forward and spat the word,

"CASA!"

The word hit Emily like venom from a cobra. It was repeated again and again,

"CASA!

"CASA!

"CASA!"

Each time it slapped upon Emily's face.

Then, she woke. She didn't scream but gulped in air with massive breaths. Sweat poured from her forehead and her pyjamas were soaked. Her knees were up to her chin and her arms wrapped around them. She looked at Ngozi who was sleeping soundlessly next to her.

Emily controlled her rapid breathing. She took a few more large breaths in through her mouth but forced herself to exhale through her nose. After repeating this a few times then she was calmer.

It was only a dream. Just a dream and nothing more. A dream which she could have described as being very vivid but there was more than that. The dream felt to Emily like a message directly from the doll.

She laid upon the pillow. She looked up at the ceiling in the darkness. After a while she leaned over the bed and lifted up her iPad. On Google she typed in 'doll island' and was amazed at the number of websites that appeared. She narrowed down her search to 'doll island mexico' and selected a few websites. Soon the story of Don Julian Santana Barrera appeared on the screen. She read his story and visited the websites offering tourist trips. She clicked on 'images' only and saw the dolls from her dream. She also saw the hut that she had been inside in her dream. It was the exact same place. Casa.

The first light of morning came creeping through a gap in the curtains. The golden light moved slowly but with purpose. When it found its way from ceiling to wall, Ngozi woke up. Emily was still staring up at the ceiling but turned to smile at her friend.

"Wow," Ngozi said, rubbing her eyes as she sat up, "I slept the whole night without waking up. You?"

Emily nodded.

"No spooky stuff?"

Emily shook her head.

"Looks like you'll be here a while then."

It was a statement, not a question. Emily was so grateful to her friend. She would stay here for a while until she worked out exactly what to do.

Ngozi rolled out of bed and picked up her dressing gown from the floor. She stumbled to the door, scratching her head sleepily. Emily sat up and pushed the pillow onto her back. She looked around the room.

Ngozi had a make-up table much like Emily's. On it was a large circular mirror. She slipped down from the bed and moved toward it. There was a word written on it in red.

'CASA'.

It had been written in lipstick. Emily heard the chain of the toilet flush. Quickly, she took out a couple of makeup wipes and scrubbed the mirror until it was clean. When Ngozi arrived in the room Emily nonchalantly dropped the wipes into the bin and put the mirror down.

"What you want for breakfast? Fruit?" asked Ngozi.

"Actually, I need to head home," replied Emily, "I need to talk to my Mum before she goes to work."

"OK. You want me to come with?"

"Nah, I'll be ok. But I'll message you later and we can meet somewhere."

Ngozi nodded. They hugged then Emily brushed her hair and packed her bag. She said bye to Ngozi's family and set off to the sound of Reggie singing in the kitchen.

The air was cold but the morning bright as she walked the streets back home. She saw several runners and a few cars setting off to work. She was lost in thought. She realised that for the first time since this had all begun, she was no longer frightened. She had a purpose and knew how to stop what was happening.

Emily walked through the door as her Mum and Paul were in kitchen eating breakfast.

"Morning!" called Paul as she walked in, "I didn't think I'd see you this early. You ok?"

She nodded and he gave her a hug before he ran off upstairs to finish getting ready.

"You sure you're ok?" her Mum asked once he'd gone.

Emily poured a glass of juice and nodded.

"I'm going to a museum today," her Mum said, "I've got a meeting to discuss loan boxes in schools."

"OK," Emily said.

"It's about an hour's drive and I don't have to go into the office."

"OK,"

"Want to come with me? It'll give us a chance to catch up. It feels like we haven't chatted properly for too long."

Emily chewed her lip for a moment.

"Yeah that'd be good," she replied, "There's something I need to ask you anyway."

Chapter Eighteen

Emily and her Mum were driving along the motorway southbound. The clouds were thick and dark, the morning air light and crisp. It was still quite early but the traffic was heavy.

Emily felt as if she was on fire. She was hot and uncomfortable and she felt that it was her world that was burning steadily. The clouds were the gathering smoke that drifted from her. Her mind was ashen and crumbling.

She had thought that this journey would be the opportunity for her to tell her Mum everything but she simply couldn't do it. The events were insane and she would sound delusional.

So, Mum, I have this doll that belonged to your dead nephew. It comes to life and runs around pushing me, scratching me and chasing me round the woods. It now visits me in my dreams and it told me it wants to go home. Do you think you can help me?

Yeah, right. How could she possibly begin?

Catherine chatted the whole way. Emily made non-committal replies. She said 'yes, Mum' and 'really, Mum' all the way down the motorway pretending to be enthralled by her phone but really, she was lost in her own thoughts.

They had all day. Her Mum had a meeting but basically this was a full day of them together. Bonding time. Catherine was worried about her daughter and this was a chance for them to tell each other what was going on in their lives. Emily would bring up the subject slowly. She would carefully unfold the narrative rather than scrunching it into a tight ball and throwing it out there as it was now formed. Hey, Mum, a doll pushed me into the river yesterday. It was chasing me and Ngozi through the woods. We were going to burn it because burying it didn't work.

Maybe not.

They turned off the motorway and onto a more rural road. They rolled over a bridge and then onward toward a small town. The museum sat magnificently on the outskirts. Emily almost gasped out loud as it suddenly emerged into view. Vast gates welcomed the car into beautiful gardens. There was a fountain with perfectly manicured bushes and a lawn that sat pristinely before the vast and elegant building.

The car was parked along a sloping road that led to the crunch of a gravel path. The revolving doors led the pair into the museum. Catherine spoke to a woman on the desk and was asked to sign in a visitor's book. She was handed a lanyard and asked to wait. Emily was busy gazing up the huge staircase and the sheer scale of the place.

"That lady said you're welcome to explore the museum while I'm having a meeting," her Mum said, smiling, "I don't think I'll be long."

"There's a trail you can do," the woman behind the counter said. She waved a piece of paper and a pencil around.

"There's one for inside and a nature trail one in the gardens."

"No, you're alright," Emily smiled back.

"You're a bit old for trails I suppose," the woman nodded.

Another woman arrived and shook her Mum's hand. They chatted for a bit while Emily continued to look around, still rooted to the spot.

"We're off to the Education Department," Catherine said, "You sure you're ok?"

"Yes, go," Emily said in exasperated tones.

Then they were gone. Emily was still standing in the same place when she realised the woman behind the counter was looking at her. She blushed a little then went off up the thickly carpeted stairs.

Her footsteps were whispers as she explored the magnificent upper two floors. She imagined herself living here wearing regal dresses and hosting vast dinner parties. The paintings in the gallery were impressive but the automaton silver swan drew her attention. It glistened and glowed in the artificial light. She saw a sign telling her that it would perform its mechanical movement at two PM.

Emily looked at her watch. It was only ten AM. She wasn't sure if they would still be there at that time. She did want to see it though.

Perhaps they could have a late lunch in the café and see the swan before they left.

There was a fashion exhibition on featuring dresses such as Dior, Chanel and Vivienne Westwood. She smiled.

Who would have thought that a trip to the museum would be such a welcome distraction to everything that had been going on? She would never have considered herself as someone who enjoyed museums or galleries or that sort of thing, despite her Mum being involved in collections. But this was exactly what she needed.

She lost herself in the exhibition imagining her strutting down the catwalk being filmed and photographed. Then back to the dressing room to hang out with Adut Akech and Natalie Ogg.

She spent quite some time looking at the dresses and displays. There was skirt worn by Kate Moss, also the 'Marilyn Warhol' dress by Versace and a variety of accessories by Yves Saint Laurent, Giles and Alexander McQueen.

Emily smiled the whole way through the exhibition. But eventually, she went off to see what else this place had to offer. If she had been told that she was coming here on a school trip then she would have been less than enthusiastic but here she was enjoying herself enormously. Not that she was about to post images on Instagram or anything. She wouldn't exactly be Snapchatting key moments from the museum.

She padded softly down the stairs and decided to see what was on the ground floor. The desk was opposite the staircase and a sign pointed the direction to the shop and café. She turned back on herself and walked in the opposite direction. Behind the staircase was more exhibition rooms. She drifted past glass fronted doors that led down to some vaults.

The exhibition she was in next featured toys from the past. She froze. The cabinets were filled with dolls. There were other toys such as bears and soldiers but Emily saw none of these. She only saw the dolls. The porcelain faces seemed to look directly at her just like the doll in the woods from her dream. She wanted to run. She wanted to leave this place and go outside. She wanted to wait for her Mum in the car. But she couldn't. A strange, morbid feeling overcame her that she needed to see them. Why? Was it like a car crash that people bizarrely slowed down to look at? Some curious fascination?

The dolls were meant to look like babies but to Emily their faces were adult. They bore worried expressions and their eyes were frightened. Some faces looked sad or lost. Some were even angry.

Emily walked closer and saw more. There was one that was meant to be smiling. The mouth was pulled back into something more like a grimace though. There were two wearing Native

American costumes who bore expressions of utter rage. It was like that were furious to be contained by the glass.

The other dresses the dolls wore were intricately detailed. Maybe that was why she found them so disturbing; it was as if they had been entombed here wearing their finest clothing. Like Kyle had been in his coffin before being cremated. He had worn a suit from a family wedding. Here, these dolls were in their best clothes and in their own glass coffins for all to see. The detail in the porcelain faces just made them look too real. Dead babies behind glass.

"You like them?"

The voice made her jump. She whirled around to see a man in a tweed suit. He carried a clipboard and pen. He was older than Paul by at least ten years, so Emily guessed he was around mid-fifties. Maybe older. His hair was grey and thinning. His glasses were quite old fashioned. He was exactly as Emily would imagine someone who worked in a museum.

"The dolls I mean."

"They're a bit creepy," Emily heard herself say.

Then she added a small and awkward laugh as if in apology for being rude. Perhaps these dolls were important to this man somehow. Perhaps he arranged this exhibition. She didn't want to offend him; he had a friendly manner.

He laughed and took off his glasses. He rubbed them with part of his tweed jacket. It actually had leather patches on the sleeves. He seemed to Emily as if he was part of the museum. A walking and talking thing from the past.

"A lot of people think that," he said with a smile.

"Do you?"

"No, I adore them."

Adore. What a funny word to use. Not like, or even love, but adore. He adored these dolls.

"Do you work here?" she asked.

"Ah, yes," he said with a chuckle, as if it was amusing of her to ask such a thing.

"I'm the Curator of Social History," he said and gave a weird little salute to her.

Then he extended a hand.

"My name is Nathaniel Winters. Pleased to meet you."

Emily shook his hand slightly.

"I'm Emily. My Mum has a meeting here."

"Ah," he said as if that cleared up the mystery of her being here.

"What does a curator of history do?"

"Curator of Social History," he corrected her, "It means I maintain these lovely artefacts and arrange for new exhibits to be displayed. There are many other pieces in storage. We rotate what we display in order to keep people interested. Keep them coming back."

She nodded.

"We also restore items. Beautifully and perfectly restored like the pieces you see here."

"I'm sorry I said they were creepy."

"Not at all," he waved her apology with his hand and a laugh, "It's perfectly normal. It is the same as a fear of spiders or snakes. A phobia if you like. In fact, the phobia of dolls is called pediophobia."

"I wonder why. Why people are scared of them I mean."

"Well, I suppose they are human-like but not quite. There's a part of our brain that tells us we *should* be scared of things, for example poisonous creatures like the spiders and snakes I mentioned earlier. A natural, self-preserving instinct, you see.

"We also naturally fear the sight of the dead. This is wired into our brains in order to protect us from contracting a disease from a corpse.

"When we see a doll or a mannequin we are seeing human like forms but they are inanimate. In that way, at first glance, the brain might mistake them for a corpse. So, our first instinct upon seeing the doll might be fear as it appears to be something that is dead."

Emily was nodding. She supposed that made sense.

"I've been given a doll," she found herself saying, "It's from Mexico I think."

It was the first time she had verbalised this. Her thoughts had touched upon it a few times. Kyle had bought this doll from his holiday in Mexico. He probably got it from some village they were visiting and thought it looked scary and creepy. He wouldn't put it on display but rather hide in a box and try to freak people out when they visited his room. He would have delighted in doing this to her. A stab of pain and loss found its way swiftly into her belly. She wouldn't ever see him again. She shook the thought away and looked at them man.

"From Mexico you say?" he said, "Beyond Mexico City there is the Island of Dolls. A whole island filled with dolls. There are lots of myths and legends associated with it including a mermaid that lures people into the water.

"But one of them says that if you take a doll from the island then you will not live to tell the tale.

"All nonsense and superstition, of course."

Emily felt as if she had a bucket of sea water poured over her. The hairs on her arms stood up straight. Shivers raced up and down her spine. That was it. Kyle had taken the doll from island. That was how this all began.

Chapter Nineteen

"Hi Emily," Catherine called out from the other end of the room.

She was with the museum woman she had gone off to have a meeting with. This woman smiled and waved at Emily. She didn't wave back.

"Making friends, Nathaniel?" the museum woman asked the curator.

"Indeed!" he replied with a smile, "Emily and I are discussing dolls and their impact on the human mind!"

Catherine gave Emily a concerned look. She had to snap out of it. She had to pretend that everything was fine. She took in a deep breath and placed a false, wide smile upon her face. Wearing a mask, she managed to speak,

"Hi Mum. How was your meeting?"

"Great! Rami and I are going to be working together a lot, I think."

The other woman nodded enthusiastically.

"What have you been up to?" Catherine asked.

"Just looking around," Emily replied.

"She's been very interested in our doll collection," Nathaniel said cheerily, "Take this for example."

He gestured toward a small boy doll with ringlet hair and piercing blue eyes.

"It features a bisque head, glass eyes, jointed composition body, fashionable costume, hand-embroidered satin, lace trim and leather shoes. It was created by Emile Jumeau in Paris in the nineteenth century. The head is made from a biscuit porcelain – ."

"We need to go, Mum," Emily interrupted.

Catherine was about to say something but then didn't.

"Aren't you going to stay for the Silver Swan?" asked Rami.

"No, we need to go," Emily said again.

Catherine was going to speak again but then didn't. Instead she sighed and nodded.

"Come on then, Mum."

Emily walked toward her, grabbing her hand.

"I'm sorry," Catherine said, "I'd forgotten. I've got to get her back for dance. Thanks, though Rami."

She looked at the curator with apologetic eyes.

"Nice to have met you."

"It was nice to meet you both!" Nathaniel replied cheerfully, "I hope to see you again at our exquisite museum soon!"

"I'll email you later," Catherine said to Rami.

She mouthed the word 'sorry' and then they were off. Emily walked at a hurried pace. She needed to think. She needed to get onto her iPad and do some searching. She needed to know more about this doll island. She went through the revolving door and headed for the car. Her Mum had to run to catch up with her.

"Did that curator say something to you? What happened?"

"Nothing, I just want to go home."

Catherine unlocked the car and Emily got in. She knew that something was wrong and suspected the curator was the cause. But she also knew when to talk to her daughter and now was not the time. She would wait until later. Probably at bed time when she took her a hot chocolate. She'd tell Paul to keep out of the way.

The journey back was in silence. When Catherine couldn't take it anymore she put Capital on the car radio to fill the car with some sound.

Emily didn't even notice. She was ordering her thoughts and reviewing all that she did know and what she wanted to know. She needed a plan and it was starting to come together.

When they got back home she went straight up to her room and opened her iPad. On Google she searched for 'doll island mexico'. Over thirty-two million hits came up. How could she not have heard of this place?

She clicked on the first website at the top of the list. It was a website offering tours. It outlined the legend and had both a photo and video gallery. She then spent time on YouTube and found over twenty thousand uploads on the subject. A lot of them were just nonsense and not related to the subject but others told different versions of the history of the island.

Emily did what she did when completing homework. She took a variety of perspectives then chose the most likely to go with. The mermaid that the curator had mentioned was on there too. But in other versions it was a giant fish.

Most websites and videos mentioned not to take anything from the island or a terrible curse would be unleashed. Some even mentioned locals taking dolls from the island and then their cars crashed.

Emily felt sick.

Just then her phone vibrated. It was Ngozi.

'u at home?'

'yeah'

'wer u been?'

'out with mum'

'comin ova?'

'can u cum here?'

'on my way'

Emily opened Snapchat to see if Meg was online. She was last seen days ago. It was so unlike her. But Emily got it. A creepy encounter with a haunted doll can do that to you. She shook her head.

She carried on watching videos and looking at images until Ngozi arrived.

"What's up?" Ngozi said as she slumped onto the bed, "Anything else happen?"

Emily looked right into her friend's eyes with a serious expression.

"Oh no," Ngozi sighed, "Did it show up again?"

Emily outlined everything that she had found out. She told her about her theory of where the doll had come from and how Kyle, her aunt and uncle came to be killed in the car crash. Ngozi looked shocked.

"So, he took the doll from the island and now the curse has been passed on to you?"

"I need to get that doll back to that island," Emily said urgently, "It needs to be fast."

"How?"

"I don't know," she sighed.

"Mexico is far away. And expensive too. My Dad couldn't believe Kyle was going."

"Do you have a better idea."

Ngozi shook her head.

"Maybe it's all finished now though. I mean last night was fine, wasn't it?"

Emily told her about the dream.

"So now its Freddy Kreuger? I said that before. We ignore it then it goes away. Right?"

It was said like a question but wasn't one.

"Where do you wanna stay tonight?"

Emily shrugged.

"I don't know," she said at last, "Here maybe?"

"You sure?"

"No. But maybe I need to see the doll. Tell her I'm working on getting her home."

Ngozi shuddered.

"I don't want to see that thing ever again."

Emily nodded.

"I know. You don't have to stay."

"I didn't mean that. It just that if you do get to go to Mexico, what are you going to do? Catch the doll and put it in your suitcase?"

"I don't know, I guess so."

She knew the plan sounded stupid and unlikely. She groaned and picked up her iPad.

"I'll do more searching."

"OK," Ngozi taking out her phone, "I'll do the same."

They were quiet for some time with Ngozi letting out the occasional,

"No way!"

After reading many variations of the same legend several times or hearing people summarising it in their own way on YouTube, Emily decided she knew the basic narrative. In some versions Don Julian was a preacher and in others he wasn't. In some the dolls were portrayed as sinister and in others they were harmless. In some the dead girl's ghost moved from doll to doll. In some there were evil spirits on the island. Sone referred to the ghosts of children killed in Aztec human sacrifice rituals.

But the story always followed that Don Julian lived on the island. He had left the La Asuncion neighbourhood of Mexico City in 1950. He grew crops and rowed a boat from his island back to the city to sell his crops. He returned one day to find a girl floating in the canal. He tried to revive her but could not. He notified the authorities and the girl was taken away. The following day he found a doll that looked much like her and decided to hang it from a tree as a sign of respect. It was then that he began collecting the dolls as he decided one was not a sufficient monument to her. He collected as many as could find on his trips into the city.

However, Don Julian then felt he was being haunted by the girl and heard the dolls whispering to him at night. He kept collecting more and more dolls and over the next fifty years collected more than one thousand five hundred dolls. It was like an obsession.

The original one he kept in his little hut surrounded by what he called 'her friends'.

Emily's involvement in this legend, she decided, began when her cousin visited the island. This was the *real* island, as many fake ones now exist as a money-making scam. Kyle probably had done his research. He would have known about these fake islands and made sure he went to the real one. He didn't tell anyone or post anything about his trip as he wanted it to be a surprise. She knew him well. Kyle would probably have planned on launching something on his YouTube channel when he got back home. That was why Emily knew nothing about it. He had stolen a doll and invoked some kind of curse. He had been killed. His parents had been killed.

Now that same stolen doll was haunting her in order to be taken back to the island. It sounded so logical and ridiculous all at the same time. She laughed. It was like a snort. An incredulous sound that something from the realms of fantasy could be happening to her. This wasn't a Hollywood film yet here she was. Stuck in the middle of the impossible scenario.

"Hey," Ngozi said, interrupting her passage of thought, "It says that in Ancient Egypt, the enemies of Rameses the third used wax dolls, meant to represent him, to bring about his death. It says dolls have always been used to bring harm to others for thousands of years. Creepy eh?"

"Like voodoo dolls I guess," replied Emily, "Where you stick pins into a doll that's meant to look like someone. Then they feel the pain."

"It also says here that something called a poppet is used in witchcraft like a voodoo doll. It's meant to represent a person, then you can cast spells and stuff to either help them or harm them."

"Great, but how does that help us?"

"It says you can get juju dolls from New Orleans too," Ngozi went on, ignoring Emily's question, "They're meant to bring good luck and protection."

"But how does that help us?"

"Well we could order one. You know, to help us. We could order a poppet or a juju doll to protect us. Fight doll with doll."

"From New Orleans?" asked Emily, "How long will it take to get here?"

"Well we could make one then!" Ngozi said brightly, "It shows you how on YouTube. You want to see?"

"Not really."

"I'm trying to help."

"I know. I'm sorry but I don't think making a doll will help us."

"Well, it's worth a try. This video makes it look so easy! I'm going to make one. All I need is some fabric, like cotton, some cotton wool for filling, needle and thread. Maybe buttons for eyes."

Ngozi watched the video intently for a moment.

"Then if I add something of yours, like a bit of your hair, then the poppet will protect you. It says use red or white material and maybe add a pattern of a shield, a key, a lock, a fence or some mistletoe."

She watched a bit more.

"Then I say, 'I have made you Emily Anderson!' and you're protected. Easy! You got a sewing kit somewhere?"

Emily rolled her eyes.

"I'll get one from my Mum."

"Some red or white material and a couple of buttons too!" Ngozi called after her as she left the room.

It was a useless idea but she might as well keep her friend distracted. After all, it was late afternoon and soon night would be here. Who knew what would happen to them that night?

This gave Emily an idea. She would set up her iPad on charge and download a CCTV app. She would record what happened to them. She would gather the evidence. Evidence she could use to convince her Mum that they needed to go to Mexico.

Chapter Twenty

Ngozi was busy sewing the fabric she had cut into a vaguely human shape. It looked like a red gingerbread man. Her brow was furrowed into deep concentration. She had cut two identical pieces of fabric and now she was stitching them together with a thin, red line of cotton. For such a small job, she was surrounded by chaos. On the bed next to her was a packet of cotton wool. Half of the contents were spilled out onto the duvet. There was also a box of buttons, also half spilled out, three spools of thread, a packet of needles and a pair of scissors.

Emily smiled. It was a useless act of utter friendship. She herself was visiting the App Store and reading reviews of CCTV apps to download to her iPad. Most of them required a camera to be added but she wanted it to be just straight to her device. She paid five pounds for iCamera Recorder and started the download. Well, it was more five of Paul's pounds as it was his Apple ID she used, but he wouldn't mind.

There was knocking at her door and her Mum peered her head around the corner.

"You've got dance in half an hour," she said.

It wasn't uncommon for Ngozi or Meg to be round when Emily had dance. Sometimes they went and watched. Sometimes they went home. Or occasionally they would just hang out in Emily's room waiting for her to come back.

"Are you going?" her Mum asked.

Emily looked at Ngozi.

"Go," she said, "I'm fine here."

"No, it's ok," Emily replied, "I can miss it this once."

Ngozi rolled her eyes.

"Go, you fitness freak. You'll only be a couple of hours. I'll be fine making this."

Emily's Mum disappeared, leaving them to sort it out between them.

"You sure?" Emily asked, "What if, you know, *something* happens?"

"It won't," Ngozi said with a sort of smile, "Just make sure you're straight back."

"OK, I'll monitor you on CCTV anyway!"

"Creepy," Ngozi said not looking up.

Emily changed her clothes to a leotard and put on leggings and a hoodie over the top. She gave Ngozi a hug and went downstairs to fill her water bottle. Paul was waiting at the door with his car keys at the ready. She gave her Mum a hug and then they left.

Catherine called up the stairs,

"Just shout if you need anything, Ngozi."

"Will do, thanks!" came the reply.

Ngozi had stitched the two legs of the poppet together. She squeezed in some of the cotton wool and pushed it down with the base of a thicker needle from the one she was using.

She hadn't noticed the scissors missing from next to her.

Then she began to stitch up the sides up to the arms on both sides. When she had finished one side using a basic but neat running stitch she reached for the scissors and could not find them. She rustled the duvet a few times and then gave up. She bit the thread with her teeth and the thin cotton snapped. The needle was threaded and she began on the other side up to the other arm.

Once both sides were completed, she stuffed in more cotton wool. The clumps she tore were too bulky to put in whole, so she shredded them with her finger nails.

Next, she began to stitch the arms. The needle was carefully navigated in and out, pushing through the rather thick red fabric.

Her face was the definition of concentration. Furrowed lines decorated her eyes and mouth. Her lips were pulled into a tight, thin line. Her stare was intently on the needle that plunged in and out of the tiny arms.

Then more cotton wool was shredded and pushed into the poppet. All that was left was the head. Ngozi remembered some Design and Technology lessons in Year Seven and groaned. How could she forget? She was meant to do the stitching and then turn the whole thing inside out before adding the stuffing. That way you wouldn't see the stich lines.

She groaned again and began pulling the cotton wool from the little doll. She wanted to do it right. It probably wouldn't work. She didn't really believe in superstition yet obeyed certain superstitious practises such as not walking under ladders, not passing people on the stairs or not opening an umbrella inside. They were just things that she did without really believing in them which was Reggie's fault. He had made her like this. He had made her, as a little girl, be wary of just one magpie and dubious of shoes on a table. He always said 'white rabbits' three times at the start of every month. It was all a bit ridiculous but she was doing the same thing now.

But, who knew? Maybe one form of superstition could stop a curse. Maybe a poppet doll could keep an evil doll away.

She shuddered. She didn't want to think about *that*.

Pulling the cotton wool out was not easy. The fibrous wool stuck to the felt fabric. She managed it though. Mostly. Then she turned the poppet inside out. She only had the head to do. Her stitching would have to be neater. There was a technique they had done in school to hide all of the stitching but she couldn't remember exactly what it was. Just the basics.

The cotton wool was pushed back inside the reversed poppet. Then she began to stitch the circular head. She slotted in more cotton wool as she went making the head plump and round.

She looked up and noticed Emily's hair brush sitting on her dressing table. Ngozi reached over and pulled some of the auburn hair free from the bristles of the brush. She stuffed these inside the poppet before sealing it shut with the last few stitches.

She bit the thread again. It wasn't quite neat enough but she just couldn't find those scissors. There was a small pair for manicuring in a pot on the dressing table. So, she got them and cut the longer hanging thread from the top of the poppet head.

There were still lots of cotton wool fibres on the surface of the doll. Ngozi rolled off the bed and slid open Emily's wardrobe. She was sure that her friend had a clothes brush somewhere at the bottom. She had seen her use it before.

There it was poking out of a plastic box that contained high heeled shoes. The last time she had seen those was when Emily had worn her favourite dress to an Ed Sheeran concert. They stood on a football pitch for hours. Emily in her green dress and matching heels had been in agony.

Ngozi shook her head with a smile at the memory and took the clothes brush to the bed. She gently brushed the poppet slicing free the cotton wool fibres with each stroke.

The clothes brush was then returned and Ngozi selected two white buttons from the bed. She sewed these on and used the small nail scissors to cut the red thread. Scooping up the cotton wool, she tidied these back into the bag. The buttons and sewing kit were also tidied into small boxes. Everything was then piled onto Emily's dressing table. Ngozi spied a Sharpie in the same pot as the nail scissors. She took it and pondered which symbol to draw on the poppet's chest. Shield? Fence? She settled on a key as she thought that this might be the easiest to draw.

The black ink tattooed the chest of the red poppet while its white eyes looked on. It made Ngozi think of some sort of weird super hero. Key Girl. With the power to unlock doors.

She capped the Sharpie and put it back into the pot. There. It was done. She held up the small doll.

"I have made you Emily Anderson," she said in a voice dripping with drama.

Then she kissed it and placed it onto the bed. Why had she kissed it? It reminded her of parties at Build-A-Bear where you had to kiss the heart of the bear before it went inside for stuffing. It was always so embarrassing and awkward.

She got up and went to use the toilet. She flicked on the light and sat down with a sigh. Everything was just so strange at the moment. What was Meg doing? She hadn't been active online since *that* night.

She washed her hands thoroughly. As if the action was somehow wiping the memory of it away.

When she returned to Emily's room a scream almost escaped her. Ngozi managed to slam her hands over her mouth so that a stifled shriek was muffled into her clamped fingers.

Wild eyes took in the scene piece by piece. Emily's green dress was now on the floor. It was cut into tattered shreds. The pieces were strewn around the room. Some pieces were on the window ledge, the bed, the dressing table, the floor. Her green heels had been snapped and thrown from the box to the floor too.

The poppet was still on the bed. Its head had been cut off.
Where were the scissors?

Ngozi stood staring at the scene. The wardrobe was still wide open. Could the doll be in there? Was it hiding behind hanging clothes clutching the scissors, waiting for her to get closer?

She didn't know what to do. She wanted to run down stairs and tell Catherine. She wanted to run from the house. Must of all, she wanted it not to be happening.

In her indecision, she heard the unmistakable sound of scissors cutting through hair. Her hair. She felt a tight tug and another cut.

She whirled around to see one lock of black hair on the floor and another drifting slowly down next to it.

She screamed and raced from the room. Her feet thudded down each step and she was out of the front door running down the street.

"Ngozi, are you ok?"

She heard Catherine's voice but didn't respond to it. She was gone.

Catherine walked up the stairs with a befuddled expression on her face. Why had Ngozi ran from the house without saying where she was going? She seemed to be in an awful hurry. Perhaps she hadn't told her parents where she was and they had called her to come back. But still, something in her urgency made Catherine want to check Emily's room. Something just didn't *feel* right.

She opened the door and peered inside. Her daughter's favourite dress had been cut up. Her favourite shoes had been snapped. Why would Ngozi do such a thing. She walked over and began gathering the shredded scraps. She piled them up angrily onto the bed. What was going on with Emily and her friends? First, Meg disappears and isn't seen. Now had Emily and Ngozi fallen out with her? It happened she supposed. Teenage girls often fell in and out friendships. She had done it herself.

Putting the snapped heels on the heap of green shreds she scanned the rest of the room. Some of Ngozi's hair was on the floor too. She picked it up and put it in the bin. Had Emily done this before she left? Is that why Ngozi cut the dress? Or had the girl done it herself?

Questions fizzed and popped unanswered. She slid the wardrobe door closed and went off for a carrier bag. She would bag up the mess and sit Emily down when she got in. They needed to talk. She needed to know what was going on with her daughter.

Catherine grabbed a carrier bag and went back up the stairs. As she was stuffing the limp pieces of dress inside she noticed a doll sitting on Emily's pillow. It was streaked with dirt and looked like the porcelain dolls from the museum.

She picked it up. The head and hair lolled backward. What was it with her and dolls at the moment too? She put it back onto the bed. She wasn't normally afraid of dolls like some people but this one was particularly creepy. Perhaps it was the mud smeared over the white face. Why hadn't she cleaned it? Why keep a dirty doll on your bed?

She left the room confused and eager for Emily to return home.

Chapter Twenty-One

Paul decided to stay and watch Emily dance. He didn't do this often but since Kyle's death he was really worried about her. She understandably was acting differently. Grief did that to you. She needed a bit of extra support and care.

He watched her stretch for a long time. She smiled and laughed with the others but this was an act. She was pretending. He could tell.

He watched the whole lesson apart from when he visited the vending machine to buy her a bottle of Lucozade Sport and some chocolate for the journey home. Some parents tried to talk to him but he wasn't in the mood.

At the end of the lesson he went downstairs from the viewing gallery and sat in his car. She hadn't noticed him watching, or so he thought, so would be expecting him to be in the car park anyway as that was where he always was.

Emily came walking out of the dance centre with a bag slung over her shoulder chatting to her friends. She slid into the passenger seat and he offered her the drink and chocolate.

"Hi and thanks," she said taking them from him.

"How was that?"

"I saw you watching. Why'd you stay?"

"It's been a while," he said starting the engine.

They exited the car park and drove the short ten-minute journey in relative silence. Paul asked a few questions but got little response so he gave up.

The car was parked on the drive and Catherine was standing in the doorway waiting for them. This was unusual and Emily sighed for a long time. Her breath was heavy to match her mood. Her shoulders throbbed and there was also a dull ache in her lower back.

"Hi, Mum," she said.

"We need to talk."

Catherine said this and walked into the living room. Paul was about to go upstairs but she added,

"I'd like you to stay."

Emily hated this. Her face reddened and her lips closed tightly shut. She dumped her bag on the floor in the hallway and followed them in. She stayed standing and found her hands clasped over her mouth. All of this because she wanted to leave the museum early? She was a bit rude, but so what?

"What happened with Ngozi before dance?"

What? She hadn't expected that.

"What do you mean?"

"She left, in a hurry and upset shortly after you did," Catherine explained, "Did something happen? Did you have a fight?"

"No," Emily replied firmly, "I'll call her now."

She took out her phone from her bag.

"There's more," Catherine added.

Emily looked up.

"What?"

"I went into your room and Ngozi had cut up your green dress. Snapped your heels too."

The words hung in the air for a while. No one said anything. Emily's brow eventually creased.

"What?"

Then Emily went to go and have a look but her Mum spoke again which stopped her.

"What's with that doll on your bed as well?"

"Ngozi made it," Emily relied, "With the sewing kit."

"I mean the porcelain one."

It was like someone had slapped Emily in the face. She looked stunned.

"What's wrong, love?" asked Paul.

She didn't answer.

"Is that the doll that was in the bag of Kyle's things?" he added.

Emily and Catherine looked at him.

"I know it's a creepy thing but it was in his case," Paul went on, "He must have brought it back from his holidays. I thought you'd know what it was. I know you and he always liked creepy stuff."

Emily had set up the iPad before she had left for dance. She needed to see what had happened.

"I cut up the dress," she said at last.

"Why?" asked Catherine in an exasperated voice.

"The last time I wore it was at Ed Sheeran. Kyle was there with his mates too. I was never going to wear it again. It makes me think of him. So, I ripped it up. Ngozi tried to stop me and we argued about it."

"Oh, Emily," her Mum said.

She went over and hugged her daughter.

"I'll call her now and apologise."

"OK," her Mum said.

Emily then went upstairs and heard her Mum and Paul whispering to each other intently.

She stopped outside of her room. The doll was in there. How did it get into the house?

It was on her bed. She held her breath. She would open the door, grab the iPad from the shelf she had left it on and go. She would lock herself in the bathroom and watch the video back to see what really happened.

She flung the door open. The first thing she noticed was that the doll wasn't anywhere she could see it. The second thing she noticed was the bag of shredded green fabric and the severed headed poppet on the bed.

Forcing herself to move she stepped into the room and reached up toward the shelf in one movement. It was gone. Her hand slowly went back to her side. Wide and wild eyes scanned the room for both doll and iPad.

She saw that it was on the floor face down. She scooped it up and ran to the bathroom. She slammed the door shut and turned on the light. Then she quickly checked the room for signs that the doll might be in there with her. She even opened the cabinets which were far too small for it and lifted the toilet seat.

She then closed the lid and sat on the toilet. She opened the iPad to see the screen had a single diagonal crack running across it.

She put in her four-digit passcode and saw that the video app was still running. She pressed the red stop button on the screen then saved the file as 'video1'. Only once it had been saved did she press the green play button.

The screen showed Ngozi sitting on the bed. Emily was changed into her leggings and hoodie. She gave Ngozi a hug and looked at the screen as she left the room.

Ngozi was intently sewing the poppet. There was no sound except for her occasional sighing or humming. Emily fast forwarded a little. Ngozi then groaned and took the stuffing out of the doll to turn it inside out. She continued working and was then opening the wardrobe and taking her clothes brush. She held the doll up to inspect her handy work. After a while Emily heard the words, 'I have made you, Emily Anderson' and then Ngozi left the room leaving the poppet on the bed.

Nothing happened, at first. Then Emily's green dress was flung from the wardrobe to the floor at the end of the bed. This was a place hidden from camera. The shoes were then thrown too.

There was the sound of cutting and a child's laughter. Then ribbons of green were thrown into the air. They looked like streamers at a party.

Emily's hands shook as she held the iPad. How could the doll throw the dress and the shoes from the wardrobe and then be at the end of the bed? The camera would have picked up the movement. As she pondered this, suddenly the screen was filled with the doll's face.

Its blank, lifeless expression looked at Emily from the past. It wasn't happening now. Yet Emily felt that it was. She felt like the doll was peering inside of her right now though. Those piercing silent eyes could read her mind and take her soul.

The iPad was then turned and thrown to the floor making the crack on the screen upon impact. Then the video was black for a long time. She fast forwarded it to when she picked it up and ran from the room.

She had saved the file. The doll's face was on there. She had evidence.

It didn't explain everything but she had something to show her Mum. But did she?

A doll's face and nothing more.

There was the sound of scissors and the iPad being thrown but would this convince her Mum that the curse of the doll was real?

No.

She used the iPad to Facetime Ngozi but she didn't answer.

Just then there was a knocking at the bathroom door. Soft and gentle knocking. She was about to call out to her Mum or Paul but she realised the knocking was very low down on the door. From about the height of a doll. She clamped her hands over her mouth letting the iPad fall to her knees.

Then there was more knocking. Louder this time. She counted the knocks. Thirteen of them.

Her armpits became damp yet she shivered as icy fingers tapped their nails all over her skin. She could call out. Shout for her Mum or Paul. Well that was in theory anyway because she found that she could not. She was trying to be completely silent. Perhaps to convince the doll that she wasn't there.

Then there was more knocking. Thirteen bangs, louder again this time. She could see the wood move on each heavy thud.

Sweat ran down from her forehead. It was difficult to breath.

There were another thirteen bangs, impossibly loud and impossibly strong. They vibrated around the room and she jumped at every one even though she knew they were coming.

"What's going on up there, Emily?" Paul called.

She heard his footsteps hitting each stair. What would the doll do now? She wanted to cry out. Warn him somehow but she couldn't find the words or her breath.

He knocked at the door. It was a very different knocking this time. Four soft taps so at stark contrast to the knocking from the doll.

She opened the door to see him holding it with a grimace upon his face.

"What's this doing on the landing too?" he asked.

He had it. He had it in his hands. It was floppy, lifeless. This was her chance.

"Could we put it in my suitcase?" she asked, as calmly as she could, "I don't want it out any more."

"I can understand that. Sure, where is it?"

"I'll get it," she said quickly, on the edges of hysteria, "You keep hold of it. Keep hold of it!"

She raced into her room and fumbled with clothes in her wardrobe. Her case was behind it. She yanked it free and almost fell backwards. She looked at the zip. There was a small padlock on it and the key was in it!

She burst out of her room and came to a sudden halt. She fell to the floor at Paul's knees, unlocked the zip and flung the case open. She looked up from the gaping case and nodded encouragingly for Paul to put the doll in.

He wore a bemused expression but did as instructed. The doll was placed face down into the case. Emily hurriedly zipped it closed. The dress, hair and tiny features entombed by the hard-shell lid. The padlock was pushed closed and she picked up the case.

"Thanks," she panted breathlessly.

"You're welcome," he said slowly, still looking confused, "Do you want anything else?"

"No thanks!" she said, a little too loudly.

Then she dragged the case into her room and shut the door. She Facetimed Ngozi again and this time she answered.

"Sorry I left," Ngozi said, "You seen your dress?"

"I've got it trapped!" Emily practically shrieked.

"What? The doll?"

"Yeah, its zipped and padlocked in my suitcase!"

"How'd you do that?"

"Come over and I'll tell you everything."

Ngozi's smile fell. She looked down and back up.

"OK," she said slowly.

"It'll be fine," Emily beamed, "I've got it trapped. It can't get out. We can stay here tonight. It'll be fine. I've got it trapped!"

Ngozi nodded and tried to smile.

"OK, I'll be there in a bit."

Emily slapped the cover back on the iPad. It was then that she heard faint knocking from inside the case. Thirteen of them.

Chapter Twenty-Two

Emily pushed the case against her bed, took her heavy parka winter coat from her wardrobe and put it on top of the case to muffle the sounds from within.

Then she went downstairs to tell her Mum and Paul that she and Ngozi had made up. She would tell them not to mention anything to her friend about the fight as it would just bring things back up again. Better to leave things as they were.

She softly padded down the stairs. Her Mum and Paul were still whispering but they had changed setting and were now in the kitchen. He was stirring a pan and she was chopping. They were silent as soon as she approached.

"Hi Mum," Emily said brightly, "What you making?"

"I'm doing a chili," she replied, "Its tomorrow night's tea. We're getting ahead of the game."

Emily nodded in reply. Her Mum often did this. She said that she slept better if the kitchen was clean and tomorrow night's dinner was done. Paul always said that it tasted better the next day too. It absorbed the flavours or something.

"Sorry about earlier," she said and hugged her Mum.

She went over and hugged Paul too.

"Sorry about everything."

Her Mum washed and wiped her hands dry.

"We're just worried about you."

"I know. I'm ok."

"You can talk to us any time, you know."

Emily nodded. Just then the front door opened and Ngozi was back.

"Bye, Mum," Emily sang and the two girls thudded up the stairs.

"Where is it?" Ngozi asked as they arrived in the room.

Emily pointed at the coat. It was like a cloak hiding a magician's box. A deadly trick was underneath.

Ngozi went over and lifted the coat.

"Don't," Emily said.

Her voice was small and weak. Ngozi turned to look at her. She held aloft the coat. The case sat beneath while she kept the coat dangling above. She was the magician revealing to the audience her greatest mystery yet.

The case thudded three times.

Ngozi jumped and dropped the coat. It landed softly and silently back onto the case.

Emily let out a sharp laugh.

"At least we know it's still in there," she said forcibly.

It reminded Ngozi of a trapped animal. Her 'sort of' uncle lived in the countryside and had once snared a fox that had been terrorising his chickens. It whined and barked like a puppy and he had shot it with an air rifle. The guts fell from its belly and its tongue lolled from its mouth. He had shown her and Adisa and been proud. They felt nothing but disgust and pity.

She felt a bit like that now. The case looked too small. The knocking had been strong though. Then she remembered the river and the dress. She stopped herself from kicking the case.

"So, are we just going to sleep in here with this?" she asked.

Emily's brow furrowed.

"Where should I put it?"

"It's locked in there, right?" Ngozi asked but went on without a reply, "I think we should double lock it."

"What do you mean?"

"Your Mum and Paul go to bed early, don't they?" again without a reply, she continued, "So when they're asleep we go downstairs with it and put in the boot of Paul's car. We set the alarm, get up early and bring it back up in the morning. Locked in the case and locked in the boot."

Emily pondered this for a moment.

"Good idea," she said at last.

Then she grabbed her iPad and sat on the bed. Ngozi sat next to her.

"Want to see what happened earlier?" Emily asked in a whispered voice.

Ngozi recoiled slightly.

"Not really."

Yet she did want to in some morbid way. She wanted to know that she wasn't going mad. Seeing it on a screen was safer in some way. It was like watching a horror film. You could look away from the screen. You knew it wasn't real. But this was reality. She would be on the screen. This really happened.

"No, I don't," she said at last.

Emily nodded and put the iPad back onto the bed. A low rumble of thunder echoed in the distance. They sat for a few moments, each lost in their own thoughts.

Emily eventually took out her phone and checked Snapchat.

"You think we should go round Meg's?"

Ngozi was looking at her own phone too. She shrugged.

"I think she needs more time."

Emily shrugged too. They both sat looking at their screens and the thunder grew louder outside.

"It's trapped, right?" Ngozi said at last, not looking up, "But what's the actual plan after that? You get it to Mexico somehow?"

Emily put her phone down.

"I don't think what I have on the iPad is enough to convince my Mum and Paul that Kyle brought a cursed doll back from Mexico and we need to take it back.

"It's trapped right now though and can't do anything to us. That's the best things have been for days. I just think we should see how tonight goes and then think again in the morning.

"I mean, maybe it can stay trapped in my case and that's that. Maybe I don't need to take it anywhere."

A clap of thunder cracked the sky loudly and near. Rain began to fall in large drops onto the roof and window. Emily got up to close the curtains. Battleship grey clouds massed in the darkening sky. A fork of white lightning flashed and illuminated the land for a second. The storm was getting closer. She closed the curtains and went back to the bed.

Ngozi looked at her doubtfully.

"What?"

Ngozi sighed.

"I don't think that's much of a plan," she said at last.

Emily opened her mouth to protest. She was angry but didn't know what to say. Her friend was right.

"I know," she eventually replied.

Catherine and Paul went up to bed not long after. The girls heard them chatting, brushing teeth and turning the lights out. After some time had passed they slid the coat off the case. There was another loud rumble of thunder. It was close now and made the lights flicker and buzz.

Emily picked up the case. It was so light but she knew the doll was still in there. She flashed a look at Ngozi. Her friend bit her lip but nodded for her to go ahead. Then she went over and opened the bedroom door.

The pair silently padded over the landing to the stairs. It was pitch black. Emily whispered,

"Walk where I do."

Ngozi nodded. They had crept downstairs countless times over the years, yet Emily always said the same thing. Whether it was when they were little, sneaking off for midnight feasts or now, hiding cursed dolls, she always said the same thing. Ngozi knew the pattern inside out. She followed Emily left, left, middle, left, right, middle, then turn for the next set and right, right, left, middle, middle, right. They were at the bottom of the stairs and both looked up.

Silence.

Paul kept his car keys on the back of his office door. Emily took them. Her Mum's car keys also had the house keys on. These hung from the locked front door. She quietly turned them and opened the door. She stepped into the porch. The rain hammered down onto the roof repetitively. They were going to get soaked through even if they stepped outdoors for a few seconds.

"You unlock the car and stay here," Emily whispered but loud enough to be heard over the storm, "I'll put it in the boot."

Ngozi nodded and pressed the keys twice. The black car flashed its orange lights twice. Emily raced out and was immediately drenched in the falling rain. Her face was scrunched and screwed up. She lifted the boot lid and saw that it was thankfully pretty much empty. She hurled the case inside and slammed it shut.

She then ran and almost slipped on the wet drive back into the porch. Ngozi locked the car and Emily locked the front door.

Her hair and clothes dripped onto the wooden floor. She put the keys back and softly padded back up the stairs to change into her pyjamas and towel dry her hair.

"I'll set the alarm on my phone," Ngozi said quietly.

"Better make it early," said Emily, "We need to get it out before Paul goes to work. You seen my hair?"

Ngozi laughed a little. They went upstairs and Emily dried her hair after they had both changed into their pyjamas. They were getting into bed when a clap of thunder rattled the house. It was so loud that it made them both jump. Emily climbed out of bed and went over to the window.

"I'll count at the next one," she said, opening the curtains, "We can see how close it is."

"Pretty close I reckon," Ngozi said, "We don't need to count to know that."

Emily looked down at the cars on the drive. She remembered the night she had seen the doll move. She closed the curtains again.

They laid down and stared up at the ceiling listening to the storm. The bedside lamp was on and neither girl seemed to want to turn it off.

Eventually, exhaustion gripped them both and their breathing became heavy. Almost simultaneously they fell asleep. Their chests rose and fell at the same time. Their nostrils flared and their mouths were slightly open. They were like synchronised sleepers.

The storm passed over as they slept.

In the morning, Ngozi's alarm sounded loudly making them both sit up. She silenced it and groaned.

"What time is it?" rasped Emily.

"Six," Ngozi croaked back.

Emily nodded and rolled out of bed. She scratched her wild and unruly hair. She stumbled toward the door. She felt thick headed. It was like the world was in slow motion. Sitting on the toilet, she held her head in her hands. Her head was so heavy. Her hair fell forward and she sat for a while.

Eventually she got up and washed her hands thoroughly and returned to the room.

"We'd better get the case," Ngozi had wrapped a dressing gown around herself and was brushing her hair.

Emily nodded through slitted eyes. Then her eyes opened slightly wider. A thought occurred to her.

"Six?" she said, "That's the first time I've slept in this house without being woken at three thirty-three."

A smile found its way upon her mouth.

"Maybe this is all over."

She put on her own dressing gown and staggered slightly down the stairs. Slipping on a pair of her Mum's shoes she stepped outside as Ngozi unlocked the car boot from the porch.

Water dripped from the guttering above the porch right down Emily's back. It made her shudder as she walked around the rain beaded car. She opened the boot and let it rise. The case was still in there. She breathed a long sigh of relief.

She lifted the light case and carried it to the house. She kicked off her Mum's shoes in the porch.

"Is it still in there?" Ngozi asked.

"Guess so," Emily replied.

She walked up to her room and her friend followed. She put the case on the floor and looked at it.

"So, what now?" Ngozi asked.

Emily looked at her. She had absolutely no idea. But they had had a successful night. The doll was trapped. She hadn't been woken at three thirty-three. Maybe this was the end of it all.

The sound of Paul's alarm sounded out from next door. It beeped several times and was then turned off. He would make tea then he would bring them hot chocolate.

"What the hell?!"

Emily and Ngozi looked first to the wall behind them and then at each other. Neither of them had ever heard Paul raise his voice before.

"Emily!" he bellowed, "Get in here now!"

Chapter Twenty-Three

EMILY PRACTICALLY RAN TO her Mum's room. What she saw when she got there made her stop dead in her tracks.

Her Mum and Paul were standing by their bed in their pyjamas. Between them and Emily was a pile of shredded clothes.

The wardrobe door hung guiltily open. Empty coat hangers hung in the dark.

The clothes had been cut by scissors. These scissors lay upon the floor. A murder weapon left at the scene of the crime. They were Emily's scissors from her room. The last time she had seen them with her own eyes was when Ngozi was making the poppet. But she had heard them from the video on her iPad. The same scissors that had shredded her own dress. She looked at the scissors then at her Mum and Paul. Their disbelieving eyes accused her of the crime. Their eyes moved slightly as if searching her expression for answers.

"Well?" Paul barked after a while.

She didn't know what to say. She made a few facial changes but said nothing.

"Why?" Mum asked quietly, "Why would you do this?"

Emily said nothing.

"I understand why you cut the dress. I didn't at first but after I've thought it over, now I do. But this?"

Emily said nothing.

"We want to help, Emily. Tell us why? We'll try and understand."

Emily said nothing.

"There's hundreds of pounds worth of clothes here, Emily," Paul now joined in, "Who's going to replace them?"

"I just want to know why," her Mum added, "Please. Just tell us."

"I don't know," she heard herself say.

"Was Ngozi with you when you did it?"

She shook her head no.

"She was asleep."

Paul made an exasperated noise and stomped off past her. He thudded down the stairs. She had never seen him look so angry.

"I think we need a night together. To talk. No going to Ngozi's and she's not staying here tonight.

"The three of us are going to sit and talk."

Emily made a barely noticeable nodding gesture.

Her Mum started to pick up the tattered shred of clothes. She had two armfuls as she walked past Emily to join Paul downstairs. She wondered if she should grab some too but decided against it.

"What happened?" Ngozi hissed as Emily entered her room.

"The doll shredded all their clothes like it did my dress," she answered in hushed tones.

Ngozi's eyes widened.

"How did it get out?"

Emily didn't answer. What would be the point? She looked at the zipped and locked case on her bedroom carpet. She shook her head. Her Mum thought she was genuinely insane, Paul wanted to kill her and supernatural forces were haunting her. She started to cry. The tears rolled down her cheeks slowly at first then the stress and the horror of the last few days came like a tsunami. She fell to the floor and sobbed an ocean.

Ngozi put her arms around her and held her. She rubbed her friends back as she let all the grief and sorrow take complete control of her. After a while the sobbing relented slightly. The endless tears became a trickle. Her hands were held over head but she released her vice grip and looked at Ngozi.

"Why is this happening to me?" she said somewhat inaudibly.

Ngozi just could find no words to reply with. The whole thing was utterly inexplicable. It just was.

Emily's Mum walked into her room without knocking.

"I've taken the day off work," she said tightly.

She saw Emily's tears but didn't go to comfort her.

"Paul will give you a lift home, Ngozi," she went on, "He's leaving for work in half an hour."

Then she left the room without another word.

Emily looked at Ngozi.

"She said you can't stay here tonight and I can't stay at yours either."

"What will you do?" Ngozi asked.

"I don't know," was the reply then Emily started crying again.

"We'll Facetime all night," Ngozi said, "It'll be just like I'm here with you."

Emily sniffed and nodded. She had to pull herself together. Perhaps it was a good thing that she and her mum would spend the day together. If anything else happened then her Mum would see it for herself. Having an adult around might be just what was needed.

She hugged Ngozi tightly for a moment and stood up. She blew her nose and wiped her tears.

"Yeah, let's do that," she said trying to sound fine.

She was doing that a lot recently. Trying to be fine. She was about as far from fine as it was possible to be. She looked at the case again then went over and shook it as if to see if it really was empty. The doll weighed so little that it was impossible to tell.

The key was on her dressing table. She wanted to check with Ngozi in the room and not when she was alone.

She unlocked the padlock and unzipped the case. She looked at her friend who nodded with encouragement. Then in one swift movement, she flung the case open. The doll was still in there. Face down. The black hair and black dress against the black lining made it look as if she wasn't at first but then tiny white fingers glowed.

Emily and Ngozi both made little gasping noises.

If the doll was still in the case then how could it have cut up the clothes? It made no sense at all.

Emily slammed the case closed. She zipped and locked it. Maybe she really was going mad. Maybe she had cut the clothes herself. Perhaps in her sleep.

Questions tumbled around her mind again and again. All had no answers.

"At least we know where it is," Ngozi said.

Emily nodded.

"I guess so."

She opened her cracked iPad and positioned it so that it was facing the case. She then pulled up the iCamera Recorder app and pressed the green button to record. Making sure the iPad was secure she turned to Ngozi.

"I'll be fine," she said, not believing her own words.

"Just Facetime me. I'm around all day and night."

"I'll probably be with my Mum being psychoanalysed all day but I'll call later. Thank you so much for everything. You're my best friend."

The pair hugged and Paul knocked on the door.

"You ready, Ngozi?" he asked gruffly.

"Oh, sorry," she replied, "Can I get five minutes?"

He made some unhappy noises and stomped off. She quickly changed out of her pyjamas, packed her bag and brushed her teeth.

"Good luck and call me if you need me. I'll still come over even if I'm not welcome but I'd better not piss him off any more right now."

She hugged Emily briskly then ran down the stairs.

"I'm ready, Paul."

Paul and Ngozi then drove off the drive leaving Emily and her Mum alone in the house. Alone apart from the doll anyway. She looked at the case, then the iPad and left the room.

Her Mum was in the kitchen. She was making scrambled eggs. There were two plates set at the table and two sets of cutlery. She meant it. She was going to be with Emily all day. What would she say to her Mum? She couldn't tell her the truth. She really would be classified as insane. She would probably get in touch with school or the doctors and arrange for counselling. Delusions brought on by the grief.

She shook her head as a firm no. The truth was out of the question. What was the truth anyway? She had no certainties. Nothing concrete to hang on to.

Perhaps the iPad in her room would provide positive evidence for her Mum but mainly for herself. That she really wasn't going mad. That she really hadn't cut up the clothes herself.

The scrambled eggs were wordlessly served up. Orange juice was poured and her Mum sighed as she sat down. Emily looked across the table at her. She had no idea what to say. Neither it seemed did her Mum.

When they finished eating Catherine looked at Emily. Eventually Emily looked back. She met her Mum's eyes cautiously, ready to look away at any moment.

"Shall we go for a walk?"

This was often her Mum's tactic when wanting to talk about difficult things. Sometimes it was a walk and others it was on a long drive in the car. It meant that they didn't need to make eye contact and if there were long pauses then it was less awkward than being face to face.

Emily shrugged a little and nodded.

"Shall we go to the nature reserve?"

"No," Emily answered a little too quickly.

She had barked the word and it had made her Mum jump a little.

"Where then?" her Mum eventually asked.

"We could drive somewhere? The beach maybe?"

"Good idea," said her Mum, standing to collect the plates, "Go and get ready."

Emily went upstairs for a shower and to wash her hair. It needed it but that wasn't why she was doing it. She would take a long time to get ready. Stall the inevitable difficult talk she was about to have.

The drive to the beach took about thirty minutes. Neither of them spoke much on the way. Catherine parked right on the sea front. The day was grey and overcast, gloomy, grey clouds endlessly hung in the vast sky above. The beach was quiet as a result of the wet weather. Their feet sunk into the clotted sand. The tide was out and the waves were far away. Their soft sound repetitively matching the pair's quiet footsteps. Salt filled the air and Emily licked her lips. It reminded her of trips to the beach during primary school. Kyle and her would be taken most days when it was sunny. They loved going to the arcades, they loved getting ice cream. They were a lot like brother and sister and it occurred to Emily that she hadn't really grieved his death. Not really. Not in any proper way.

The doll had consumed her attention utterly and it was only now that she had arrived at a place that she associated with him that she realised how much she missed him. The grief came tumbling down upon her as an avalanche.

She stopped and started crying. Her Mum held her close and she cried too. They remained like this for quite some time.

"I just miss him so much," Emily said at last.

"I know," her Mum whispered back, "I do too."

Catherine had lost her sister. A sister she was close to. They live mere streets from each other. They had spoken on the phone pretty much every day since childhood and saw each other a few times a week. They had both drifted apart when they had been at their universities but since settling back in their home town, the closeness had returned.

Emily realised at that moment how hard this all must have been on her Mum. She held her tightly and knew that the last thing she could do was tell her about the doll. She had to be strong and deal with this herself. She had to be strong for her Mum.

The difficult talk Emily had been expecting never arrived. Instead, after they had hugged for a long time, they spent the day as if nothing had happened. The clothes were never mentioned.

They had a fish and chip lunch wearing rain coats and sitting on a bench overlooking the damp sky and brooding sea. They played air hockey and shot hoops in the arcades. Then, later in the afternoon they held hands as they walked back to the car. Both felt better for the time away from the house. But sitting in a corner of Emily's mind was the doll. Sat watching and waiting for her return.

Chapter Twenty-Four

Emily didn't want to go up to her room. She stayed with her Mum and helped her make dinner. She chopped potatoes into small pieces for mash while her Mum cut up chicken breast getting rid of any bits with veins and things in. The potatoes were set to boil so Emily cracked three eggs into a bowl. Her Mum poured breadcrumbs into another bowl and set it next to the bowl of breadcrumbs. Emily dipped the chicken pieces into egg, then into the breadcrumbs and finally a frying pan with a little oil.

The chicken nuggets were fried then put into another bowl lined with kitchen roll to soak up the excess oil. Sweetcorn was roasted in the oven.

This was a meal that Emily's Mum had made her since she was little. It was pure comfort food and they both needed it.

Paul walked through the door. They heard him inhale deeply and they both smiled.

"Fried chicken!" he declared, "Love it. I thought we were having chilli?"

"It's in the freezer," Catherine replied in a loud voice, "We needed comfort food."

He hung his coat and walked into the kitchen. He paused there and looked at them both.

"We good?" he asked.

Emily went over and hugged him. She didn't say anything but he hugged her back. Then her Mum joined them and the three of them hugged in the kitchen.

They ate at the dining room table chatting about this and that. Despite the normality, the doll was an omnipresent figure for Emily. It was in her room but also in her mind. She pretended and she distracted herself but there it was. An ever-present resident. A persistent presence that nothing could exorcise. The thought that continually reoccurred was 'what's going to happen tonight?'. It was like the waves from the beach. It came and went repetitively. She could be thinking or talking or listening and there it was again and again.

What's going to happen tonight?

It was a whisper of smoke that drifted lazily here and there.

What's going to happen tonight?

It was a stab from a knife that sliced through everything else.

What's going to happen tonight?

It was the buzz from a wasp hitting a window, trying to get out again and again and again.

She shook her head. It was all out of her control. The iPad was in her room recording. The doll was in a suitcase trapped and yet inexplicably not.

"Emily."

Maybe she should check the iPad and review what had happened today?

"Emily."

But she didn't really want to. Maybe she would before bed but for now she was enjoying this. She needed the normality just having dinner with her family presented.

"Emily!"

"What?" she asked.

Her Mum was leaning right over to her.

"Paul was asking you about today," her Mum said with eyes that suggested she was being rude.

"It's ok," Paul smiled, "I just asked who won at air hockey."

"Who'd you think?" Emily grinned back.

"Yeah," Paul went on, "Only because *I* wasn't there."

"Next time," her grin widened.

"Hey, hadn't you better get ready for dance?" her Mum said, also smiling.

Emily looked at the clock on the wall and then her watch. She nodded and pushed back her chair.

"We'll leave in twenty," Paul said, collecting dishes.

Emily went upstairs and paused at the door. She closed her eyes for a moment. She steeled herself then pushed it open. The suitcase was sitting innocently on the floor. There was no sign of disturbance or violence. No destruction.

She grabbed the iPad and ran to the bathroom. Then she changed her mind and went to her Mum's room.

She pressed the red stop, green save file then green play. Her finger controlled the speed of the playback. Nothing. For the whole entire day. She let out a long and loud breath of relief.

She set up the iPad to record again after she had changed for dance. She wore a leotard with leggings and a hoodie over the top, her usual attire. Her bag had a drinks bottle and a purse with a few other random things like bobbles, chewing gum and a small mirror.

Her eyes kept flicking back to the suitcase. Her ears were fixated on it too. No knocking, no whispering, nothing. Maybe this was it? Maybe it was all over? She didn't really believe that and gave the suitcase one last look before she left her room.

Paul was waiting by the front door, keys in hand. Her Mum was loading the dishwasher.

"Bye, Mum," she called as they left.

They drove with music on and Emily noticed that Paul stayed for the lesson again. He was worried about her, she knew that. She was worried too.

The dance lesson worked as distraction for a while but then it was over. When she went outside it was really raining. What was going on this summer? Raindrops the size of large peas hammered the cars. The sky sounded like a waterfall yet there weren't any individual clouds in the sky. It was all just a vast ceiling of grey and it was darkening by the second.

She pulled up her hood and they both ran for the car. They were drenched instantly. The car fogged up as soon as the doors were closed. Paul started the engine and put the AC on. The sound on the roof was loud and persistent. Emily heard what she thought was thunder but it turned out to be a passing aeroplane. She didn't like the thought of air travel in this weather. But perhaps the plane was above the clouds so it didn't matter.

It was down here on the ground were things were bad. The roads were covered in about an inch of water. Paul drove slowly, carving two lines through the water. Someone walked along the pavement nearby. His hood was up and he carried two plastic bags with milk bulging from both. Paul purposefully slowed down so as not to further drench then man.

As they neared home the rain lessened slightly. The beat upon the car slowed down to a rhythmic tap, tap, taping instead of a bang,bang,banging. They slowed down again as he crept the car onto the drive, the lights illuminating the side of the house and the lines of rain between.

Emily ran inside but she was soaking anyway. She stood in the porch dripping. She took off her shoes and hoodie. Then, with wet socks called out,

"Hi Mum!"

She went straight upstairs and despite being soaking, she still paused briefly before entering her room. Then she stopped. The case was open on the floor. The doll was nowhere to be seen. She stepped forward slowly and peered around her bed, under her dressing table, at the closed wardrobe.

She looked back at the case. It was laid upon the floor, wide open with two gaping mouths of black lining. There was a knocking at her door which made her jump. It wasn't the doll's knocking though. She knew that knocking. She could instantly recognise the sinister savagery the doll's knocking projected. This wasn't Paul light tapping either but rather it was her Mum's 'I'm coming in' knocking.

She attempted to compose herself and made her mouth change shape into a smile.

The smile instantly dropped to the floor as her Mum entered her room holding the doll. She had it cradled like a baby in her arms. The hair hung down covering her elbow. The head was turned toward Emily. Those blue eyes drilled into her. The painted mouth looked to be smiling.

"Why did you put this on my bed?" her Mum asked.

A million thoughts collided with each other all at once.

"What?" she asked, stalling to regain composure.

"This was on my bed. I assume you put it there?"

"Of course."

"Why?"

The question was light and airy but also wasn't. Emily knew her Mum was worried about her for all sorts of reasons. Sure, putting a doll on her bed wasn't as crazy as cutting up clothes but it was still strange behaviour.

"Do you think its creepy?" Emily asked.

"A bit, why do you?"

"Yeah, I was just wondering. You can leave it in that case if you like."

Her Mum's brow furrowed. Then she put the doll in the case and looked at Emily.

"You ok?"

Emily nodded and managed a smile.

"Paul stayed for dance again," she said quickly attempting to change the subject.

"I know. He's worried about you too."

"We'll get there."

Her Mum hugged her.

"Can you make me a hot chocolate, please?"

She nodded and left the room. Emily instantly slammed the case shut then zipped and locked it.

Grabbing the iPad, she pressed the red stop, saved the file and watched back what happened. There was nothing but then she saw the case fall on fast forward. She paused it, went back and watched it again.

That was it. It just fell. It didn't open. Nothing came bursting out. Could this thing teleport its way from one place to another?

She fast forwarded again and saw little fingers emerge from the zip. White fingers creeping from the darkness within. They split the zip apart and pushed. They moved slowly and carefully. Then the screen went dark.

She checked that it wasn't her iPad locking itself. It was the video playing back still. The darkness remained as she fast forwarded some more. Then the screen lit up. It showed her room and the open case.

She stopped the video and ran her hands through her hair. It could get out. Whenever it wanted to. The case couldn't trap it. Nothing could.

There was her Mum's knock upon the door. She came in holding the hot chocolate.

"Are you ok? You look very pale."

Emily focused her attention on not letting her hands shake as she took the drink from her Mum.

"Yeah," she managed to say.

Paul tapped at the door and stepped inside.

"I've set up Connect 4 downstairs," he said, smiling, "Thought we could have a game. Winner stays on."

"Connect 4?" laughed Catherine.

"Yeah, it's been a while but I thought it might be fun."

"Good idea," said Emily, welcoming the distraction.

She walked past her Mum and up to the door where Paul was standing.

"Come on then," Emily said smiling and pushing past him.

"Aren't you going to get changed?" Paul asked, "You're still dripping wet."

She looked down at herself then back to him. He had changed into tracksuit bottoms and a new T shirt.

"Oh yeah," she said limply.

Paul and her Mum left her room so that she could change. She could hear them whispering about her as they went down the stairs. She closed the curtains and put on pyjamas while watching the case. Then she went downstairs.

The remainder of the evening was spent with popcorn and playing Connect 4. Emily kept getting beaten as she was so utterly distracted.

"You're rusty," Paul said, "We need to play more often to get your game up."

She had smiled back at him and grabbed some popcorn. The minutes became hours and all the while the doll was waiting in her room.

After she'd brushed her teeth, Emily said good night to her Mum and Paul. Then she climbed into bed and Facetimed Ngozi. She answered after two rings. Emily saw that Ngozi was in bed.

"You ok?" her friend asked.

"No," Emily replied honestly, "The doll can get out of the case. It was on my Mum's bed."

"No way! Well, I'll stay connected all night. We can get though tonight and work out a plan tomorrow."

Emily nodded. She wanted to change the subject. She wanted to talk about something, anything else. She could see the case in the corner of her eye. She could keep an eye on it and that was enough for now. She didn't want to talk about it anymore.

"You heard from Meg?" she asked.

"No. Shall we go round tomorrow?"

Emily shrugged and nodded again.

Then the iPad fizzed and crackled. The screen faded to black. She tried turning it back on but it wouldn't work. She put it on charge but nothing happened.

She grabbed her phone and Facetimed from that. It rang once then it too faded to black and was dead. Then her lamp crackled and went out. She was in complete darkness.

Chapter Twenty-Five

EMILY JUMPED FROM THE bed and went to flick on the light switch. She took care not to trip on the case or even touch it. She pressed the switch several times but nothing happened. She left her room to find Paul standing in the dark on the landing.

"Whole house is tripped," he sighed, "I'll get my torch."

He fumbled his way back into his room then came back moments later with the massive torch. Emily could see its vast, baseball bat like outline in his hand. The beam of the torch flicked over her. She stayed on the landing, unwilling to go back to her room unless there was light.

He thudded down the stairs, the torch light swaying this way and that. Then the lights suddenly came back on. They buzzed too brightly at first and then returned to their normal glow.

Paul looked up at the light, turned the torch off then resumed his journey to check the trip switches in the garage. Emily remained on the landing waiting for him.

"You ok?"

Her Mum had her head peering round her bedroom door. Emily smiled and nodded back.

"Did he fix them?" she asked, "What was wrong?"

"They just came back on by themselves," she replied.

Just then, Paul's footsteps were back ascending the stairs heavily.

"Dunno," he announced, "Everything's fine."

Emily went back into her room. The ceiling light was on, her bedside light was on, the suitcase sat innocently by the bed. She went and checked her phone and iPad. Dead. They didn't have a landline phone anymore. She would be on her own tonight.

She looked back at the case. Not quite alone.

Sleep was out of the question.

Perhaps she would sneak downstairs when her Mum and Paul were asleep and watch TV quietly with the lights on.

Yes, that would be her plan. She read a book for a while but her eyes kept on finding themselves drawn to the case.

It had been difficult choosing the book too. She wasn't a person who had many books on the go at once. She read one book at a time. The one she was currently immersed in was The Girl With All The Gifts by M R Carey. She had read it before. She had read the sequel, The Boy on the Bridge, and his other book, Fellside, too. Her current read was the second time for her. She didn't do that very often but it was such a superb story. A zombie book with a completely different feel. It was raw yet beautiful. It had been in Kyle's bag of possessions too as she had bought for him for Christmas.

She didn't want to read that tonight. She wanted something comforting. Something familiar yet something she hadn't read for a long time. She took Skellig from her shelf. She loved that book and hadn't read it in years.

If only her encounter had been more like this. If only the thing in the case had been more angelic than sinister. Although was Skellig angelic? Michael could have been as terrified of the figure in the garage as she was with the doll in the case. He had been brave. He had not turned away but rather faced his fear.

Maybe she should do the same?

Maybe all this time the doll behaved in the way it was being treated. Like a child. Thinking about the events of the last few days, was it not the behaviour of a spoilt child taking tantrums and playing silly tricks? There was nothing actual evil in what had happened. She had been pushed into a river and her dress had been cut up at worst. Weren't those the acts of a ruined child lashing out with anger at not getting their own way?

Maybe she should take the doll out of the case, hold it in her arms and talk nicely to it. Was that all this would take to make it all stop?

But it was out of the question. She just could not do that. What if it turned its head to look at her? What if it scratched at her again?

People with a fear of spiders had arachnophobia but what had the curator said a fear of dolls was? That was what she had whatever it was called. If she didn't have it before then she certainly had it now. Could someone who was scared of spiders cradle a tarantula in their arms? Cuddle it and say lovely things?

She tried to read again but find she could not. She was just too distracted. Looking at the clock it said ten forty-five. She would give it another forty-five minutes to make sure her Mum and Paul were asleep then go downstairs.

Sighing, she got up and decided to do her nails. She got everything ready; polish remover, file, scissors, nail strengthener and a new burgundy colour. She looked up at her mirror.

"Fake tan tomorrow," she sighed.

She looked so pale, like the ghost of her former self. Working on her nails and frequently looking at the case, the time eventually passed.

She listened with her ear pressed against the wall between her room and her Mum's. She thought she could hear Paul's snoring. They seemed to be asleep.

Emily wrapped her dressing gown around her. Despite it being summer, they did live in the North of England and it was cold.

She followed the familiar pattern down the stairs; left, left, middle, left, right, middle, then turn for the next set and right, right, left, middle, middle, right. Looking up, the light from her room glowed but there were no sounds at all. She went into the living room, turning on the light. Then she pushed the button for the TV and held the remote. There would be an initial blast of noise but she had her finger on the volume button ready. She just hoped that that first burst from the TV wouldn't wake them upstairs. Her Mum's room was right above the room she was in.

Luckily, it was a documentary on the TV and not some raucous action film. The sounds were pretty quiet to start with and Emily made them quieter still. She scooped up the Apple TV remote and turned it on. Selecting Netflix, she settled onto the sofa, snuggling into her soft dressing gown. Her eyes kept creeping to the door to make sure she wasn't joined by the doll.

She flicked through films and TV shows and finally settled on A Series of Unfortunate Events. She had read the books when she was younger and loved them. There had been a film ages ago but she hadn't loved that. This was probably a bit young for her and that was perfect. The title had drawn her in. This was what the past days – *had they really only been days?* This was what it had been like for her; a series of unfortunate events. She would take tips from the Baudelaire siblings. They always used intelligence to overcome difficulty, she could remember that from the books.

The series turned out to be brilliant. She lost herself in the narrative of the short episodes utterly. It was during the third or fourth that the lights fizzed for a moment or two and went out again. The TV had gone off at the same time.

She sat, alone in the dark. She pulled up her knees and squeezed the dressing gown in her hands. Paul was now asleep. He wouldn't appear in the door with the torch in his hand ready to do battle with whatever. Her eyes adjusted to the darkness and scanned the room.

She had to move. Violet Baudelaire would not just sit there like some damsel in distress. She stood up and tried to think if there was another torch somewhere. But first, she knew it was useless but she flicked the lights on and off a few times, just to be sure.

Then she padded over the floor to the door. She peered up the stairs. It was immersed in utter darkness. She felt the wall and traced it to the downstairs toilet. There was a torch in the cabinet under the sink, she was sure of it. Behind candles, cleaning products and toilet rolls, there it was. She turned it on. The batteries were low but it worked.

She had seen Paul flick the switch in the garage to return light to the house before. She used the weak torch as the guide back along the corridor, into the kitchen and then on into the garage. All the while she was conscious of checking for anything else in the house. Anything that moved. Anything that wasn't her Mum and Paul.

The torch found the box on the wall to the left of the door. The black switches were all raised which meant that they were fine. The fault was nothing electrical. Perhaps more *supernatural*?

She stepped back into the kitchen unsure of what to do. The torch scanned a little way ahead but the dim yellow light was growing dimmer. She needed to decide. Should she wake Paul? Should she go upstairs or stay down?

The torch weakly shone up the stairs. Maybe she should find a better torch. Perhaps that should be step one. She opened the cupboard under the kitchen sink and let the light scan in there. She kept turning to look behind her too, listening intently in the dark too.

She did find a smaller torch but at least it was a bright LED one. She put the weaker torch into the cupboard and closed the cabinet door. The torch practically lit up the whole kitchen. She nodded. One step at a time.

So, what was next? She shone the torch around the room and caught a glimpse of something moving that was not in the room with her but rather was something that was on the stairs.

She flicked the torch back in that direction and lit up the bottom few stairs. The doll was standing on the third from bottom step. Its face stared at her through the torch light. The light wobbled as her hands shook. She used both hands to steady the torch. They remained frozen like this. The emotionless doll simply staring and standing, the frightened girl unsure of what to do next. Emily fought to keep the torch in one place. It was almost as if she had the doll trapped in the light like a tractor beam from a UFO.

Time passed slowly. Despite its small size, the torch felt immensely heavy in her hand. The doll's relentless staring drained the energy from Emily. The beam of light began to shake and fell ever so slightly away from the doll. It had been a fraction of a second. Less even. Then she had the light back on the little porcelain figure. Only now it was on the bottom step. It was closer to her.

Emily took a step backward. She concentrated hard on keeping the light firmly fixed in place. But the doll's stare was unyielding. It went on and on. Its eyes were a bottomless cavern.

The torch wavered, just a fraction again, but then was back. But the doll was closer. It was on the wooden floor close to the kitchen door. She could close the door but it would mean her walking toward the doll. It would mean getting very close to it and Emily just could not do that.

In a slight twitch, a muscle spasm in her hand, the torch wobbled away and returned. Now the doll was inside the kitchen.

It stood on the floor looking up at Emily who was pressed hard against the kitchen sink. The option of closing the door was now vanished. Her hands shook uncontrollably now. With each shake the doll drew nearer and nearer.

Chapter Twenty-Six

IT WAS GETTING CLOSER to her. Emily's hands were wildly shaking now both in fear and fatigue. Her grip was tight but the muscles in her fingers protested as to how tight they were. As the torch bounced around the doll inched slowly toward her. It moved in flashes, like a strobe light. When the light wasn't on it, it got closer. She didn't actually see it move. Its stuttered approach was one of those flip motion books. When it was half way across the room she let out a blood curdling scream which seemed to spring her limbs to life. She turned and ran to the living room slamming the door closed behind her. She leapt onto the sofa and whirled the torch back toward the door. But the lights were on. So was the TV. Count Olaf was menacing the Baudelaire children. Sweat beaded on her forehead and she looked around the room with wide and desperate eyes. Her chest heaved in and out.

"What's wrong?"

Paul was there, with his torch.

"Are you ok, Emily?"

Her Mum was there too. Both worried. Both looking around the room for what could be wrong.

Paul turned off the TV and Catherine sat next to Emily with her arms around her.

"The doll!" Emily heard herself scream.

She pointed toward the kitchen but she already knew there was nothing there. She looked at her Mum, then at Paul and finally at the TV. She's fallen asleep. But then why was the torch in her hand?

"I've been dreaming," she sighed, "Sorry. I fell asleep. A nightmare."

She stood up and wobbled uncertainly. She steadied herself. She was a dancer. Core strength was something that she had an abundance of. Taking in a long and deep breath she looked at the pair and managed to wear something like a smile.

"I'll go back to bed," she went to brush past them but the lights flickered and hummed.

She stopped. Her eyes widened and looked at Paul who still held the torch.

"Come in with us for a few minutes," her Mum said, "Do you want a hot chocolate? It might help you sleep."

Emily nodded. She and Catherine went upstairs and Paul poured milk into a mug. He heated it for one minute and ten seconds. One minute wasn't enough and one minute twenty was too long. He was really Goldie Locks about his hot chocolate. Then he added two spoonful's of Nesquik and stirred for a long time. Emily pictured the scene as it happened. It brought her comfort.

She hugged her Mum in bed and Paul arrived with the drink. He slid in beside them and Emily sat up to sip the hot and chocolatey milk.

Had she dreamed the scene? The torch was in her dressing gown pocket as a reminder that she had not. Well, had she dreamt part of it at least?

The hot chocolate was gone before she knew it. Paul took the mug and put it on his bedside table next to his pint of water for the morning. He always drained the glass before getting out of bed.

She sighed and sat back. The three of them had their heads on the large, soft headboard. What would she do now? She guessed that she would go to her room, wait for them to fall sleep and watch TV downstairs again. She would try her iPad and phone too. But then the doll was in her room.

As if summoning something by her thoughts, the two bedside lamps hummed and grew dimmer. Then they flashed brightly and went out.

Paul's torch was on. He flashed it at both lamps then leaned over to flick his on and off. Then he stalked over to the main light switch and pressed that a few times.

"Must be a power cut," he sighed.

There was the giggling of a small girl. He whirled around with the torch in the direction it had come from. Emily shrank back toward her Mum.

It had come from the door. He stepped toward it and onto the landing. Then the giggling was in the room. Emily closed her eyes and grabbed at her Mum. Paul was back in the room with the torch. He moved it around the floor in swift motions.

The giggling was back outside again. He whirled around and moved toward it. Then he tried the main light again a few times. Giggling sounded out from Emily's room. He slowly stepped from the landing and into her room. The beam of light from the torch slid over every surface. Until it found the bed. Sitting innocently between two pillows was the doll.

Its white face was turned toward the door. Toward Paul. The blue eyes were locked in place staring at him unflinchingly in the light. He moved toward it. The torch fixed on its face.

He shook his head. The torch flicked around the room again. But when it returned to the doll, the thing was now stood up. He jumped a little. What the hell? How could that have happened?

How could it be standing anyway? The head was way heavier than the rest of it. The tiny feet couldn't support it.

He held the torch in place for a moment or two then moved it away but still kept looking at the doll. It was immersed in darkness but he could make out the silhouette. A tiny child of darkness in the black air that surrounded it. Nothing, at first but then it moved.

He flashed the torch back at it. It was closer to him. It still stood on the bed but was now standing on the duvet and not next to the pillows. Morbidly and perhaps somewhat fascinated he moved the torch away for a moment and then back. The doll was closer.

What was he doing? What was it doing? How was it doing it? He had to know. He had to be sure that this wasn't just some trick of the mind in the dark. That this wasn't just some conjuring of the imagination. Or Emily's imagination.

This whole time. Had it been a *doll* making her behave so crazily? He moved the torch and stepped backward, toward the door, a little.

When the light returned to the porcelain figure it was at the edge of the bed, closer again.

He turned and raced back to his room. He flicked the main light a few times and then did the same at the nearest bedside light.

"What's happening?" asked Catherine, "Did you check the trip switch?"

There was that same taunting, childish giggle again. Paul whirled around with the torch and the doll was standing in the doorway.

"What's that?" asked Catherine.

Emily grabbed onto her and moaned.

The beam of light from Paul's torch wobbled with uncertainty. He was scared. He looked back at the pair in the bed. Then his brow furrowed. It was a doll. It was a fraction of his size. Moving or not this was ridiculous.

He strode forward with wide strides, keeping the doll in the torch light. Then he grabbed it roughly in one hand while holding the torch in the other.

There was a sharp sting of pain. He dropped the torch and then the doll.

"Argh," he cried out.

He felt warm liquid run down his arm. There was metallic tang in the air. He scooped up the torch that was still rolling on the carpet and illuminated his arm. Blood flowed freely down his wrist. A long cut ran diagonally.

He flicked the torch back to the floor. The doll was standing. Standing holding a pair of scissors that dripped blood silently onto the carpeted floor.

He flashed the light back to his arm. It wasn't that deep but it hurt and was still bleeding. When the doll was back into the light it had moved forward again with the scissors gripped in one tiny, white porcelain hand.

Paul turned and ran to the bathroom door.

"Quickly!" he barked.

Emily and her Mum flung the duvet off and jumped to the en-suite. Paul followed them in and slammed the door shut. His back was against the wood and he dripped blood onto the white laminate floor in the dark room.

"Hold this," he said gruffly holding the torch for Emily.

She took it and held it as steadily as she could. Her Mum wrapped a white towel around Paul's forearm that soon turned red.

She snatched the torch back and opened the door.

"No," whispered Emily, "Don't."

The doll was still standing on the carpet at the other end of the room. It still held the scissors but they no longer dripped. They were stained in Paul's blood though. Some of it was visible on the black dress too. Spots of red that were fading into the fabric by the second. The expressionless face looked on. White and devoid of all emotion.

Paul framed the doll in the light. He took an uncertain step forward.

Then the ceiling light and the bedside lamps glowed a dull orange colour. They made angry buzzing sounds. Emily and her Mum stepped out of the bathroom to see what was going on.

The lights began to flash brightly, like they were photographing the room. They buzzed and flashed again and again and again. The room was lit by the strobe lighting momentarily then plunged into darkness repeatedly. It disorientated all three of them but their attention was fixed upon the doll.

It began to move forward with each second of darkness. They didn't actually see it move but with every second of light the approach was illuminated. A freeze frame, step by step, steady flow of movement.

The doll carried the scissors in one hand menacingly, its face never changing, getting closer and closer. Then the scissors were in both of its hands. They opened and closed as it approached. The sound of the lights flashing on and off were mixed with the sound of slicing. Metal slid smoothly over metal again and again. Chopping neatly and with a deadly menace.

Paul turned and pushed the pair back into the bathroom. He slammed the door shut and slid the lock. The light in there also flashed on and off in vivid brightness but as soon as the door was shut and lock secured then it went out.

Now there was darkness and the sound of heavy breathing. Paul was crouched with his back against the door. Emily and her Mum were also crouched but kneeling against one another.

Then there was knocking. Three light taps against the door. It made Paul jump and recoil. He leaned in to the others.

The bathroom was silent and still. All three held their breath, waiting for what was next. More knocking? The door handle turning? It bursting in?

There was scratching. Light scratching of metal against wood. The scissors were being scraped up and down the door on the other side.

Then banging. Not knocking. Not the light three taps from before but rather a hammering of heavy fists that made the door bounce and shake. Emily counted. Thirteen of them.

She sobbed. There was fear but something else too. There was a slight sense of relief that she wasn't alone. She clenched on to her Mum and Paul.

There was a pause and then the banging came again. And again. Always thirteen knocks. It wasn't possible that a tiny doll could make such loud noises upon the door. The sounds were immense and filled the room entirely. But then none of this was possible.

Another thirteen knocks. Then another.

Paul stood up. He held the torch like a weapon. He steeled himself and grabbed the bolt of the lock between thumb and forefinger.

"No," Emily said again.

He pushed the bolt back and then held on to the door handle. He breathed in quickly and deeply a few times and then flung the door open.

Chapter Twenty-Seven

As soon as the door was opened the lights came back on. They didn't flash and weren't too bright, they were just right. Normal and without noise. He let out a quick burst of breath and stepped out into the bedroom. He then squatted quickly to check beside the bed and was off to check the rest of the room. He looked to Emily like a SWAT team in a movie.

"In here!" he called.

Emily's Mum stood up and she did the same. They crept cautiously from the bathroom into the bedroom. They went on in the same slow pace, clutching each other to the source of Paul's voice. They paused on the landing though.

"In here," he called again, quieter.

He was in Emily's room. The main light was on. So was the bedside light. On the bed. Laid upon a pillow, was the doll.

It stared up at the white ceiling. Its motionless face seemed to Emily that it would spring to life at any moment. That it would turn to face them and snarl. That it would jump to its feet brandishing scissors.

As if hearing her thoughts, Paul pointed to the pot of make-up brushes on her dressing table.

"Look," he said.

In the pot were the scissors. The scissors that had been in the doll's hand not long ago.

Emily's eyes returned to the doll. Then she saw the case with the split zip. What would they do with it? What would be the point anyway? Had the doll hidden the scissors in her dress? It was utterly pointless guessing the logic behind such a thing, Emily knew that. There was no reason. There was no behavioural pattern to follow. There was no logical path.

"Your case is cut," Paul said, reading her mind again.

He bent down to examine the slice of the thin fabric.

"Let's use mine then."

Then he swiftly left the room. Emily and her Mum clung to each other a little tighter as he left. They continued to stare at the doll. It was as if looking at it might keep it fixed in one place. It made Emily think of the Weeping Angels on Doctor Who. She didn't watch that show much but she liked the episodes with those in it. She had like the episode that Neil Gaiman had written too about the Cybermen. The Weeping Angels reminded her of the ghost on the beach in M R James's 'Oh Whistle and I'll Come To You My Lad'. She shook her head. Why would she be thinking of that right now?

Paul returned with a grey, hard shelled case. He put in on the floor next to her case wide open. He took in a sharp breath then grabbed the doll and in one swift movement, he had it face down in his own case. The brightly coloured electric blue and white lining was at stark contrast to her own case. The raven hair of the doll spilled in every direction. Had it been growing? It looked longer to Emily than it had been when she had very first seen the doll.

Her eyes squinted and she leaned forward. Had nails grown on those porcelain fingers too?

Paul shut the case and zipped it closed. Then he sat it upright and pushed a silver padlock through the holes in the zips. He locked it and stood upright.

"Right," he sighed, "It might not work."

He shrugged.

"Shall we go down stairs and talk about what the hell that was?"

Without waiting for an answer, he thudded down the stairs. They heard him turn on every light; kitchen, dining room, living room, hallway, downstairs toilet, porch.

The pair slowly walked down stairs. Paul was sat on the sofa in the living room. Catherine joined him. Emily squeezed herself in the middle.

It poured from her. After one deep breath, the whole series of unfortunate events burst forth.

"It started when I got Kyle's bag of things. I saw the doll, it looked creepy but I didn't think much of it. Then weird stuff started happening. It pulled off the duvet in the night, pulled at my hair, scratched me.

"I thought I was going mad. I told Ngozi and Meg. So, I put it in the wheelie bin outside.

"The next night, it was out and standing on the drive. It looked up at me."

She stopped and started crying a little. Paul was stroking her back. Her Mum held her hand. Their eyes were wide and they said nothing.

"So Ngozi, Meg and me, we buried it. Over at the nature reserve. We took it in a bag and buried it.

"But that night. It came back. So, the next day, we went back to the nature reserve to check and it was gone. I haven't seen Meg from around then I think. I don't know. It's all just a big blur into one now. Well, Ngozi and I were in the woods and it was there. It chased us. It was in front and behind. It chased us down to the river then it pushed us both in. Well, it pushed me in and I fell onto Ngozi.

"That was when I broke my phone and took your spare."

She said this to Paul and he nodded back to her. Her Mum had an expression of utter confusion on her face. Not just about the phone, which she didn't know about, but rather about the whole thing. Her mind just couldn't process what her daughter was telling her. Pieces of an impossible puzzle were fitting together though. Unexplained behaviour from her daughter was becoming clearer in this insane explanation.

"We came home but the doll did too. It was on my bed. But then you got it in my case. I thought that was it. It was trapped. But then it cut up my dress. I've got it filmed on my iPad. I downloaded a CCTV app and filmed it."

She went to stand up in order to get her iPad from her room but then changed her mind.

"It broke my iPad though. It cracked the screen.

"Then it cut up your clothes. It must have kept the scissors. It cut its way out of the case and did those things tonight too."

Her explanation was disjointed. She wanted to add other pieces that she had remembered like the knocking at the bathroom door that Paul had heard. Or them going to burn it at the nature reserve. She wanted to tell them that Meg had disappeared. Ngozi had been an incredible friend. She wanted to explain why she had acted to weirdly at the museum. Why she had acted so weirdly this whole time.

But then she stopped talking and started crying. The tears fell from her as her Mum and Paul held on to her. She could tell they were looking at each other. Communicating in some way either through mouthing words and gesturing somehow. But she didn't care. The stress of these days was lessening slightly. She had unburdened herself. Ngozi and Meg knew what had gone on. Well, Ngozi anyway. But it was different telling her family. She felt as if they could do something. Then she remembered that she had missed out the writing on the mirrors and her dream. Casa.

"We need to take it back," she said looking up through tear streaked, blurry eyes, "It's the only thing that will make this all stop. Kyle took the doll from an island in Mexico. It needs to go back. The doll is cursed."

"Mexico?" Paul said, "We can't go to Mexico."

"What do you mean?" her Mum asked.

"I've found out all about the doll," Emily explained, "I've done research. Ngozi too. Kyle went to the Island of Dolls near Mexico City. He stole the doll from there. He brought it back but its cursed.

"There are stories about people taking dolls from the island and being killed in car crashes."

Catherine shook her head. This was too much. Her sister hadn't been killed by *a doll*.

"What do you mean stories?" asked Paul.

"Some man called Don Julian collected dolls on an island. He found a drowned girl and she had a doll with her. Well, something like that. Anyway, he then started collecting dolls. The island's full of them. You should see the images and videos. A whole island filled with over a thousand dolls.

"People now visit it as a museum or something. And we need to go there. We need to take the doll back or what happened tonight will just keep on happening. It doesn't end. It won't stop unless we stop it."

She started crying again. Paul stood up and came back moments later with a box of tissues and his laptop.

"What's it called?" he asked.

"What are you doing?" Catherine asked.

"Checking it out," he replied.

She gave him an incredulous look as he opened the laptop. Emily wiped her tears with a tissue and said,

"Pass it here."

He slid the laptop over to her. The adults either side leaned in as she typed 'doll island mexico'.

She showed them images first. The decomposing and dirt strewn faces of dolls appeared. Their lifeless eyes similar to that of the doll upstairs. Then there was an image of Don Julian himself staring up at dolls hanging from ropes in the trees. Cobweb covered faces and decapitated heads decorated the trees. Lifeless plastic limbs hung limply from boughs and branches.

She then clicked on Trip Advisor reviews and pointed to the screen. Her Mum and Paul leaned in closer to read. After visiting several websites, Emily then typed in 'doll island Mexico legend' and visited a few websites that pretty much told the same tale.

They all read the screen in silence. After a while Emily typed in 'what happens if you take a doll from doll island mexico'. The only results that came up where ones that said that people often took dolls to the island, not the other way around.

Eventually though, Emily found a website that told a story of some locals that had taken a doll and died in a car crash but this was vague. Where had she read this before?

She stumbled across another doll island called Nagoro in Japan. She also found a doll called Robert from East Martello Museum in Florida. People visited the doll in the sailor suit that lives inside a glass case. Emily thought that this would not be enough to contain the doll that was upstairs.

She continued to click on websites relating to the Mexican doll island. She pointed out that there were fake islands that were easier to get to.

"But we need to go to the *right* island," she said, "If we take it back to a fake one then it won't work. We'll still be cursed."

"Cursed?" her Mum asked, shaking her head, "What are we doing here?"

"Did you not see the *doll moving*?" Paul gasped angrily, "Look at my hand!"

He held out the blood-soaked towel wrapped around his hand.

"I don't want to believe it either," he said a little calmer now, "But that doll was alive just now. It was alive and was trying to hurt us.

"Everything Emily has told us shows that a suitcase isn't going to hold it. We need to get rid of it."

"Then we'll throw it into the sea," Catherine said, "We'll burn it."

"I already buried it," Emily said quietly, "It came back."

Paul suddenly stood up.

"OK," he said, "OK, let's burn it. Right now. In the garden."

"I don't think – ," Emily began but he was already out of the room.

His footsteps thudded up the stairs and he was back moments later carrying the suitcase.

"Paul, I don't think – ," Emily said but he was ignoring her.

He slammed the case onto the living room floor in front of the sofa. He took the tiny key from his pyjama pocket and fiddled with the padlock. Then the zip was yanked downward and the case lid lifted open.

The bright lining seemed to jovially mock their wide eyes. The case was empty and the doll was gone.

Chapter Twenty-Eight

Emily wasn't really surprised. She had more than half expected the doll to not be there.

"Where's it gone?" her Mum gasped, "It was in there. It was definitely in there."

Paul balled up his hands into fists. He made an incredulous noise and punched the wall nearby.

"My room," Emily whispered, "I'll bet it's in my room."

She silently left the room and went up the stairs. Did the lights flicker as she ascended or was it her imagination? Probably her imagination.

Her legs were dead weights. Paul and her Mum followed her behind. She had them and now nothing could scare her. She wasn't insane.

Her stride became more confident. She pushed open the door and there it was. Laid upon the bed, head resting on the pillow, eyes up at the ceiling.

Emily turned to look at Paul and her Mum. Their stare drove straight past her and found the doll. Her Mum let out a little frightened startled gasp. Paul was shaking his head.

"That's it," he said, "Emily, can you take it downstairs?"

Her confidence fell. It tumbled away like a papier-mâché costume. It had been a thin and false thing anyway. She looked at her Mum who stood there with her hands clenched against her jaw.

"No."

She heard herself say. Paul nodded,

"OK. Wait for me in the living room. Both of you."

Emily took her Mum's hand and they went back downstairs. Paul went into her room. She looked at her Mum. She was a ghostly white colour. Seeing her like this only made Emily regain her composure. She wanted to be strong for her Mum. This must have been what it was like for Ngozi. Her friend had been a rock for her. Down at the river had been awful yet Ngozi had just carried on being there for her. She could have just left, like Meg, but she didn't. She had no obligation to be any part of this. Yet she did this out of pure friendship and loyalty. Emily owed her big.

Now it was her own time to step up. Her Mum was clearly shaken by the whole experience. Who wouldn't be? It was time for her to be the strong one.

Emily took her Mum's hand as they wordlessly walked to the living room. Should they sit? Stand? She ended up rolling up the blinds and looking out into the garden. The patio doors were black rectangles of ink and all she saw was her own reflection looking back at herself. She wanted to turn off the lights so that she could turn off her reflection.

Paul thudded into the room clumsily but with purpose. The doll was in one hand. He didn't carry it to his side but held it in front of him like he was making sure it didn't disappear from his hand. Or keeping an eye on it to see if it *did* anything.

In his other hand was a box of matches and some lighter fuel that they used to refill the lighters for the many candles in the house. She wondered why the matches and not one of those.

"I'm going to burn it," he announced, "It will all be over soon."

She unlocked the patio door that Emily stood by and went outside. He slammed the matches and lighter fuel onto the step and strode toward the shed. The doll bounced here and there in his hand.

Emily followed him outside and her Mum joined her, glued to her side. They stood on the step, next to the matches, to see Paul emerging from the shed with his fire pit. It was actually a washing machine drum he had recycled into something that could be used as a fire pit. It certainly wasn't one of the sunken posh ones she had seen on TV but it did the job.

He placed it on the stone path that led from patio doors to shed cutting through the grass that sat either side. Then he looked at the doll. He paused momentarily then put the doll in the metallic drum. Emily picked up the lighter fuel and matches. She nodded and even managed something that resembled a faint smile as she handed them to him.

He squirted the lighter fuel. Emily stepped forward to see the dress being soaked and then the hair. Some of the liquid splatted on to the porcelain face too. It ran down her cheeks like streams of tears. Once the bottle was empty he flung it onto the grass and clutched the matches determinedly.

Her Mum joined her now. They both looked down at the little doll in the dress. It was such a sad sight but neither did anything to stop Paul. He struck three matches all at once and dropped them into the drum. They landed on the wet black dress and with a little humphing sound ignited into bright yellow flame. The whole doll was then instantly engulfed with fire.

All three of them took a step forward to watch. To make sure the thing didn't leap from the flames and return to the house. To make sure it stayed where it was, burning.

The flames had now covered the figure from head to toe. The dress, the hands, the toes, the face, the hair; all alight.

After a few moments, an expression of confusion found its way over Emily's brow. The hair. It was human hair or something similar. Horse hair perhaps? She remembered the texture of it in her hands. She had compared it at the time to the dolls she had held. She had always found dolls creepy yet had owned a few when she was little. There were the Monster High dolls but they really didn't seem to Emily like dolls at all. They were so plastic and the hair was so fake. She didn't mind those. Other dolls from her childhood had been the same. All plastic with synthetic hair. Maybe that was what she found disturbing about this doll. It was too realistic. It was like a small child. Now this small child was being burnt in her garden.

But it wasn't. The hair should have disappeared by now. She remembered holding out a pulled strand of her own hair into the fire one night while toasting marshmallows and watching it vanish immediately with a slight sizzle. She, Ngozi and Meg then took turns with several strands at a time from their hair brushes one night in this very garden and with this very fire pit.

That seemed like an age ago. She peered into the flames further with narrowed eyes. The entire doll was alight but not burning. The porcelain face blankly looked beyond the fire.

The hair and dress should have gone by now. They had been soaked in lighter fuel yet remained intact. The flames engulfed her entire frame yet nothing changed.

The three of them looked on and then looked at each other. Their faces flickered orange along with the hungry flames below. They looked back to the doll. It still sat surrounded by the fire. How was this possible? How could it be burning?

Paul held out his hands to the fire. It was certainly hot. He waved his fingers over the flames and then returned his arms uselessly to his side.

"What do we do?" asked Emily.

They wordlessly looked at one another. Catherine then turned and went back in the house. Paul and Emily joined her. She closed the patio doors and then locked them. The lights were then turned out and they stood by the window watching the flames rise and fall from the drum.

"It'll burn out," Paul said at last, "It has to."

"Then what?" asked Emily.

He didn't answer but walked to the sofa and flipped open the laptop.

"What are you doing?" asked Catherine.

"Looking at flights to Mexico," he replied with a furrowed brow staring at the screen.

His face was lit up by the white glow of the laptop. He looked over at Catherine and Emily. Their faces were lit by the orange flames from outside. He shook his head then started tapping at the keys on the laptop.

"Fifteen hours from Newcastle," he said, "One stop. In Amsterdam."

"You're not being serious," Catherine said walking over to him, "How much is that?"

"A thousand pounds."

"Each?"

He nodded.

"We can't afford that," Catherine said in an exasperated voice, "Are you being serious?"

"Its three thousand pounds or that!"

He practically screamed this. He was stood holding the laptop in one hand and had a finger pointing to the window.

"That doll stabbed me!" he screamed again, "It can't be buried or burnt! It can't be trapped! It can move by itself! This is the only way!"

Emily looked at him then back outside. The flames were dying down. They were smaller than before but still visible.

"I've watched horror films!" he went on, "Mostly with Emily, so she knows this!"

"Knows what?" Emily asked.

"That everyone makes stupid moves," he sighed, calmer now, "They do the wrong thing. But this?"

He looked at the laptop then back to them,

"This is our only play. This is our only option. We take it back then it all goes away.

"This is the *non-stupid* thing to do. I know it makes no sense. I know it seems mad. But there is a doll that can't be burnt in our garden. There is a cut upon my hand. They are just plain facts."

He paused as if to let his words sink in.

"We've only experienced this for one night," he directed this at Catherine, "She's been coping with this for days."

He put the laptop down and went over to Emily.

"I don't know how you've done it," he said to her, "I don't know how you've coped but I'm so proud of you."

He hugged her and she wanted to cry.

"This is insane," Catherine said, "There must be another way. We can't afford it."

"I'll find the money," Paul replied quietly.

He was still hugging Emily and looking out at the dying flames.

"I have to."

Then he unlocked the door and went over to the drum. He reached into the fire pit and picked up the doll. Smoke rose from it in tendrils that coiled lazily into the air.

"It's not hot," he said, "It's as cold as before."

He shook his head slightly then placed the doll back into the drum.

"I can't explain it," he said walking back toward the house, "I can't explain any of it. It makes no sense but I think it's the only plan we've got."

We scooped up the laptop when he returned to the house. He started tapping at the keys again.

Catherine and Emily watched him for a while then went and sat next to each other at the edge of the sofa. They watched the smoking doll outside without words. Neither of them knew what to say or what to do.

Emily thought that Paul was right. She did know that.

She also had another feeling. Now that the decision was made, now that they were actually going to take the doll back to her home, they were no longer in danger. The doll had got what it wanted. It somehow didn't seem sinister or threatening any longer. It was calm and content.

She didn't know where that feeling had come from but she knew it to be true. This wasn't anything that she could explain in logical terms out loud or even in her head in any orderly way. But rather it was just a feeling that had settled upon her. She looked at Paul. He slapped the laptop closed.

"We fly tomorrow night," he said, "We're going to Mexico."

Chapter Twenty-Nine

THEY DIDN'T GO TO sleep that night. They booked a hotel for two nights, sorted the airport transfers then packed a few clothes. All the while the three of them kept looking out of various windows into the back garden to see if the doll was still there. It was.

"It's a night flight," Paul said to Emily on the landing, "So plenty of time to get sorted."

It was like he was telling himself more than anything else. Like he was reassuring himself of the timescale when realistically she could have had a bag ready in minutes. But in whose bag would the doll go? Hers. It had to be hers. The doll had called her name and her name alone. This was a curse that had been put upon her for whatever reason. However unreasonable, however unfair it was, that was the fact of it. This was happening to her right now. The fact that her family was helping her and her friends, well friend, had helped her, was comforting, but this was down to her.

She left her room and went downstairs. She looked out from the patio window. The fire pit drum was sat on the grass that needed cutting. It was a dull summer morning. Grey clouds filled the sky entirely. Birds, in particular pigeons, flapped this way and that but other than that the garden was entirely still. There was no movement from the doll at all.

She unlocked the door and went outside. The chill morning air filled her nose and then chest. It felt good. But only briefly. Soon, the cold filled her frame. She stepped toward it. Toward the doll. It was inside the fire drum surrounded by grey ash from previous fires. It stared up at the morning sky with a face like a mask. Who knew what was going on behind those frozen blue eyes. Not Emily. She did wonder if the doll thought. Did it have a consciousness of a sort? What was it thinking right now? What did it know?

She *felt* that it knew that they were going to take it home. Casa. Back to Mexico. She *felt* that the doll would now not be threatening though. She didn't know it to be true but she *felt* it.

Looking down at it now, she didn't feel the same fear of before. She felt something that resembled fear, certainly, but it was heavily mixed with pity and sadness.

She picked the doll up and brushed grey ashes from its dress and hair. From *her* dress and hair.

Turning the doll this way and that, it maintained its fixed stare ahead. Emily brought it toward her and stared at the smooth, dirt stained skin and ruddy red cheeks. The lips were thin yet perfectly formed. The eyelashes and eyebrow colour were exactly matched to the dark hair. It wasn't black she now noticed but rather a very deep and dark brown. The dress was black though. A midnight ink colour. The colour of a raven's eye. The white frills on the collar and sleeves were perfectly stain free. They were at stark contrast to her hands, feet and face.

Emily took the doll back inside and placed it upon the kitchen counter. She took a pack of wipes from the cupboard under the sink and pulled two free. She slowly, carefully, wiped the dolls porcelain face. She checked to see if the antibacterial wipes were rubbing off any part of the painted features but they were not. She cleaned the face so that it glowed white with healthy red cheeks either side. Then she brushed the hair, first with the tips of her fingers and then with her whole hand.

Taking the doll upstairs, she slid open her wardrobe and found the clothes brush. She brushed down her dirty, stained dress. The soil and ash fell into her bin and onto the floor.

With her hair brush, she gently brushed the hair again. A mere day ago this would all have been impossible. Yet, here she was pampering the thing that had terrorised her for what seemed like so long. Terrorised her not hours before.

Emily knew that if Ngozi saw her now, then her friend would have thought her insane. But her actions didn't feel insane. They felt like exactly the right thing to do.

When the doll looked like its former self; before the burying and burning that is. Emily placed it upon her bed. Pride of place.

She then checked her iPad. It turned on. The Apple symbol glowed on a black background. The screen then illuminated. There were twenty missed Facetime calls from Ngozi. She smiled. She had a good friend who was worried about her. But everything would be fine. She was taking the doll to her home.

Looking at her clock Emily saw that it was seven AM. They would go to the airport later that afternoon. About five PM Paul had said. Off to Amsterdam then an overnight flight to Mexico City.

She had always wanted to go to Amsterdam. She had heard about the shopping in Mexico City from people at school; Antara Fashion Hall, Downtown Shopping Centre, Sky Mall. But she really wasn't bothered about any of these things now. She was on a mission to take the doll back and that was that.

For an hour or so she packed her bag. She couldn't use her suitcase as the zip had been cut. She pushed that under her bed to be binned later. Instead she used a holdall she used to use when she was little.

The bright red fabric was a little stained and there was a Top Model badge sewn onto it but she didn't care. She also didn't care about what she was packing.

After the hour, she called Ngozi. Her friend answered after just one ring.

"Are you ok?" Ngozi said breathlessly, "I was about to come round."

"Thanks," Emily smiled, "I'm fine. My iPad died but seems ok now."

"Yeah but is everything ok?"

Emily nodded and smiled. She turned the iPad toward the doll on the bed. Ngozi made a gasping noise. Emily turned the iPad to face her.

"It's ok," she smiled as Ngozi's shocked face, "It's ok."

"How?"

"My Mum and Paul are taking me to Mexico. Tonight. We're taking the doll back."

She spent around twenty minutes explaining, as best she could, what had happened last night. Ngozi listened and stifled her questions by literally biting her lip until Emily had finished. She did her best to explain how she now felt about the doll but knew that she didn't really have the words.

"This whole time she's behaved like a child. A child who wants their own way."

"What do you mean?"

"Scratching, pulling hair, pushing. It's all a tantrum. She wanted to go home and that it."

"What about cutting up clothes? Chasing us through the woods?"

"It's something a spoilt child would do."

She winced at her words and looked at the doll. She didn't want to offend her.

"Why do you keep calling it a *her*?" Ngozi asked, "It's a thing. A scary thing. You are talking like someone in a film. You're being ridiculous."

"No. I'm doing the opposite of that. I'm being real. This is the only way. We're taking her back."

"Throw it in the river. You've got it now. Tie rocks to it and throw it in the river. Or better, the sea."

Emily shook her head.

"This is happening. I'll call you."

She wanted to stop talking like this in front of the doll. She would talk to Ngozi properly when she got back. When it was all over. When her friend could see that she was right.

"I've got to go," she said, sighing, "I'll message you."

Ngozi went to say more but Emily ended the call. It stung to treat her friend like this. Ngozi had been amazing. She would make it up to her. But she needed to do this first.

The doll stayed inanimate. It looked comfortable, happy even, but perhaps this was Emily's imagination.

She took a shower and washed her hair. When she was back in the room the doll was in the same place. She dried her hair and straightened it. The doll was still there. She started sorting her clothes and wash bag. She shoved them into her holdall. The doll was still there. She hadn't moved. This was what she wanted. This was what she had wanted all along.

Emily nodded. The doll was happy. She was going home.

They had checked in online already so it was just a case of dropping off their bags then taking the short flight to Schiphol, in

Amsterdam. Fifteen hours on a plane were after that. Emily had not been on such an epic journey before. She had downloaded things form Netflix to her iPad but knew that she wouldn't watch them.

Placing the bag onto the floor as they stood in the line she looked at it. The doll was in there. She had put her between clothes so as to protect her. She had folded a hoodie as a pillow. She had even spoken to it.

"We're taking you home," she had said, "I've got to put you in this bag but you're on your way home. Everything will be ok now."

She had closed the zip on her bag. It had reminded her of a detective show on TV. She had examined the victim and then closed the body bag. Her holdall was a body bag. It didn't seem right to be checking it in.

"I think I should put the doll in my hand luggage," she said, looking at Paul.

He looked at her for a few moments.

"OK," he eventually replied, "If that's what you want to do."

She squatted to unzip her red holdall. The doll was smothered by her clothes. She slid her out carefully and then placed it in her handbag. It was a Ralph Lauren that she had bought with Christmas money in the Boxing Day sale from John Lewis. It had her purse, phone, iPad, charger and a makeup bag in it and that was all. The doll poked from the top. Its head fully exposed. The people who had joined the queue behind them stared at the doll and then at Emily with curious expressions.

She didn't care. Let them look. What did it matter?

They checked in their bags then went up the escalator to go through the security checks. She wondered briefly what the staff would think of her carrying a doll as hand luggage. They wouldn't confiscate it for some reason, would they? Then she shook away the thought.

She placed her iPad, phone and purse into a tray then the bag onto a different tray and went through the machine that checked for metal. She didn't beep. She then stood waiting for her things to come through the machine. Two staff members pointed at her doll. They looked at her then the doll then back to her.

Snide comments would follow but she didn't wait around for them. The three of them, four if you included the doll, went for a drink. She couldn't be bothered to look around the shops. What was the point? She had a job to do and that was that. There would be time to return to normality later. This wasn't a holiday. This was something that resembled a mission.

They boarded their first flight to Amsterdam. She kept the handbag under her seat. She was going to store it in the overhead compartment but it felt wrong to lock her away in the dark.

Once they landed they walked quite a distance through the vast airport to the transfer desk. Again, there was more security. A Dutch security guard picked the doll out of her handbag and said something to his colleague. They both laughed as they looked at her.

"Quite a traveling companion!" he exclaimed to her.

She smiled and said nothing back.

They made their way to the gate for their flight to Mexico. It wasn't for another two hours but they sat at the gate waiting anyway. No one else was there and they didn't speak. They were on their way to Mexico. The doll was going home.

Chapter Thirty

The night time flight was long. No one spoke. There was nothing to say. Not until the doll was safely delivered and they had a long way to go yet.

Emily was exhausted but she couldn't get to sleep. The hum of the aircraft and movement all around her made it impossible. But that wasn't it. The doll under her seat was what it was in reality. She lost herself in the events of the past few days. How many had it been? She tried counting backward but everything had become one long blur. When was the last time she slept? It certainly hadn't been last night. It was night time now and still sleep would not come.

She looked over at Paul. He was snoring lightly and was leaned against her Mum. She squeezed Emily's hand and smiled. The smile was weak but genuine. Her Mum smiled back and mouthed 'you ok?'. Emily nodded.

She ended up putting in headphones and watched the tiny screen for a while. She started at least three films but couldn't get into anything.

The flight was impossibly long. It was freezing cold too. She had expected to be hot and sweaty but the air conditioning was set up to maximum and she shivered beneath a thin blanket. How could people feel comfortable in such conditions? It wasn't just

Paul who slept. Most of the passengers were dozing in their chairs. The flight went on and on.

Finally, they landed. The hot South American heat hit her the second she stepped from the plane. They filed toward a bus. It was a hot and humid afternoon. The bus did not have air conditioning. The heat was stifling and invasive. She hung on to both Paul and a metallic pole as they zig zagged a crazy route toward the airport from the runway.

Thankfully it was over and they ascended an escalator toward baggage reclaim. They joined more queues for passport control. She had stopped noticing the stares and comments about the doll. She was too exhausted to care. Miraculously, they got through the security checks pretty quickly.

"Good job we didn't need visas," Paul said to her Mum.

Emily didn't know what he meant and couldn't be bothered to ask. They left the cool of the airport and entered the heat of outside. Sweat beaded on her forehead immediately. She had been to hot countries before like Spain and Portugal, but she had never felt heat like this. It was damp and sticky, moist and roasting all at the same time. She felt her armpits dripping and inwardly groaned.

There was a long line of yellow taxis. It reminded Emily of a scene from New York. Paul leaned into a window and asked for the price to take them to Xochimilco. Where they going straight to the island now? She had assumed that they would be checking into the hotel and going tomorrow.

She looked at her watch which had collected a band of sweat underneath the white plastic strap. It was two PM local time. Maybe there was time to take the doll back this afternoon. Whatever the cost to the pier to catch a boat was, it must have been fine because the driver was now out of the car and lifting their cases into the back.

Their cases. How could they take a little boat to the island with suitcases? Their cases weren't big. After all they were only here for less than a week and had hurriedly packed, probably inappropriately too.

She squeezed herself into the back next to her Mum who was in the middle. She then leaned over her to ask Paul,

"Are we going to the island now?"

He nodded seriously.

"I've booked a hotel near to the Xochimilco pier," he explained, "We can check in now and then head to the pier."

She nodded back too and leaned back into the car seat. It had a clear plastic cover that made her sweat even more. The air conditioning was on but the driver had his window down that let in the hot and humid air. The bright sun baked her skin through the glass next to her. The window revealed huge roads with gigantic prehistoric looking tropical trees that lined both sides.

It was only a thirty-minute journey but it seemed to last nearly as long as the flight. At last they arrived at Hotel Amala. It was painted in gaudy colours; orange, pink and turquoise. Its curved walls went up five storeys. They pulled up beneath a blue neon sign.

Paul had collected the pesos at Newcastle airport. He now paid the taxi driver and must have tipped well as the driver practically hugged him while he shook his hand vigorously. The cases were lifted from the boot and then the driver was off.

The hotel staff were friendly. They smiled warmly and asked questions about where they were from, how the flight was, where did they plan to visit while they were here but then these questions abruptly stopped. The receptionist was staring at Emily's bag. She self-consciously shifted it round to her side.

Not another word was said by the young woman. She handed Paul two plastic key cards and pointed to the lift behind.

He thanked her and the three of them wheeled their cases away from the desk. Paul pressed the button and the lift door opened immediately. They stepped inside and pressed he pressed the number three. The doors slid silently shut.

"You'd better put that thing in my backpack," he said as they ascended, "Did you see that woman's face when she saw it? I'll empty my bag when we get to the room."

Emily nodded.

"Yeah, good plan."

She didn't like him calling the doll a thing. She wasn't really sure why though. She had called it 'a thing' herself, she was certain of it. But not anymore. Now it wasn't 'a thing' at all. Now it was . . . What was it? What had it become? Not a little girl. But certainly, something that was alive in some way.

They walked down a grey carpeted corridor with white walls. The inside was such an opposite to the outside. They arrived at their rooms and saw that they were next door to each other. Paul handed Emily a key and she pressed it against the lock. It flashed green and made a small beeping noise.

"We'll give you a knock in five minutes," he said.

She nodded in reply then went inside. She realised that her Mum had not spoken at all since the flight. She would need to talk to her on their way to the island. She would need to see if she was ok.

The room was turquoise and white. The double bed had a turquoise neon light running around the base. She dumped her handbag on the bed and used the toilet. The bathroom was bright and clean. It was mainly white but the turquoise theme continued. She wondered if the room next door was the same.

She washed her hands thoroughly using lots of lemon scented soap. Then she collected the doll. She didn't need anything else. She realised that she hadn't even turned her phone on since getting on the first plane. She didn't need it. She wanted no contact with anyone, not even Ngozi, not until she had taken the doll back to her home.

She slid the key card into her leggings pocket and left the room. She knocked at her Mum's room and Paul answered.

"Almost ready," he said and she followed him inside.

The theme in here was red and white instead of turquoise and white but the décor was exactly the same. The red light glowed at the bottom of the bed.

Her Mum emerged from the bathroom. She looked pale and exhausted.

"We can take a boat from the pier opposite the hotel," Paul said, "We'll probably need to be quick if we're going to make it today though. On the websites I looked at most of the tours leave in the morning. We might need to do a bit of bribing."

"We can just go tomorrow, you know," Emily said.

"No, we can't."

Her Mum's voice was hoarse and rasping. The circles under her eyes were large and dark.

Emily nodded. Her Mum needed the doll to go now. She understood. Maybe, after the doll was back, they could actually relax. They would sleep in these large, colourful beds and be better tomorrow. They were here for a week. It might turn into a real holiday. But first they needed to get this done.

Paul had emptied his backpack onto the bed. Emily put the doll inside and slowly zipped it shut.

"I'll carry it," she said to Paul.

He smiled and nodded. Then the three left the room and took the elevator back down to the reception desk. The same woman was there. She coldly regarded them as they left the cool of the hotel and entered the heat and humidity of the afternoon sun.

Paul was right. The pier was directly opposite the hotel. They crossed at a set of traffic lights. The pier was lined with extremely colourful canal boats. They had red seats on board beneath painted roofs of many colours.

"We need to get the right island," Emily said.

"I know," said Paul.

They approached a group of men who were sitting on small plastic chairs and smoking cigarettes.

"Hi," Paul smiled at them.

They looked up.

"Si, senor?"

"We need to get to the doll island. Not the fake one but the real one. The one Don Julian first lived on."

"I can take you tomorrow senor," one of them replied, "Not now."

"I can pay," Paul added.

"Tours are morning and evening only," the same man said, "Sorry, senor."

"I'm after a private tour. Just the three of us. But it's got to be now."

The man shook his head.

"Sorry, senor."

The men started talking to each other in Spanish and ignored Paul who stood there for a few moments. Then he went back over to Emily and Catherine.

"It's normally up to two thousand pesos for a tour. Should I offer four thousand?"

"How much is that?" asked Emily.

"About one hundred and seventy pounds," he replied.

"Just pay it," Catherine said firmly.

Paul sighed and nodded. He went back over to the men and said,

"I'll pay three thousand pesos for a tour now."

The men looked up.

"Five thousand," a different man replied.

"Three thousand five hundred."

The man shook his head.

"Four thousand," Paul said after leaving a small gap in the haggling.

The man rubbed his chin for a moment.

"OK, we go now," he said at last.

"But it has to be to the original island. Don Julian's island. Agreed?"

"Si, si."

Paul turned to Emily and Catherine who were already walking over.

"How long will it take?" asked Paul as he handed over the money.

"Three hours," replied their newly employed guide, "One hour there, same back and an hour on the island. Sound ok?"

"We won't need an hour on the island," Catherine snapped.

The guide shrugged and set off to a boat along the line. Emily realised that the boats all had names painted onto the roofs. There's was called Lupita.

The outside of the boat was red and was painted yellow inside. The back of the boat had no side, the base of it lay on the surface of the water and that was where they stepped on board. They ducked under the Lupita sign and sat on little yellow chairs that sat beside a long red and yellow wooden table that ran the entire length of the deck.

Their guide had a long oar like the ones used in the canals of Venice. After untying Lupita, he pushed the oar into the water. Then he shoved at the canal floor and effortlessly slid the boat away from its neighbours.

They were on their journey to the Island of Dolls.

Chapter Thirty-One

Emily looked at her watch. It was nearly four PM. They would be on the island by five. The guide pushed the boat along the canal gondola style. She didn't know when it would get dark in Mexico. She hoped it would be after they returned to the pier.

The dark water barely made a ripple after each push of the long oar. She leaned on the yellow topped table with the red trim. The chair she sat on was small and uncomfortable. This was yet another part of this epic journey she was on.

Car, plane, plane, plane, car and now boat. All to return a haunted doll back to its home. How many miles had she travelled? She had no idea. Paul probably did but she couldn't be bothered to ask him.

She remembered that she was supposed to ask her Mum if she was alright but silence seemed to settle comfortably upon the boat which suited her just fine. That was until the guide began something that sounded like a monologue spoken many times before.

"Welcome to the Xochimilco canals," he said with no emotion at all, "These canals stretch on for one hundred and seventy kilometres. They were given World Heritage Site certification in nineteen eighty-seven. They are an area of natural beauty.

"First formed in the tenth century by the Aztecs, Xochimilco is a floating garden. They were made by constructing reed rafts with mud and clay from the bottom of the canal. They were then attached with roots from the ahuejote trees which are native to this area. With the nutrients from the lake they have grown their own vegetation and are now solid, as islands.

"The Aztecs were farmers and grew beans, maize and other things on these mineral rich islands. The canals through the islands on this lake became a trade route for many years.

"The Spanish and Portuguese explorers known as the Conquistadors that came to South America not only brought an end to the Aztecs but also to life as Xochimilco knew it.

"Many battles were fought on these islands and the bodies and blood of Aztec warriors are sunken below these waters.

"There are stories of ghosts that haunt the islands. Not just of Aztecs but others too."

Emily found herself intrigued, despite her fatigue. She leaned on the table. Her head cocked slightly to one side to listen more intently to the guide.

"La Llorona known in your language as the Weeping Woman haunts these waters," he went on, "She was a beautiful woman called Maria. She was married with two children. But her husband left her for a younger woman. So, in revenge she drowned her two children in these waters. After she had done so she realised what she had done and then drowned herself. She drifted up to Heaven and St Peter asked her where her children where. She came back to Xochimilco to find her children and that is where she has been ever since searching for her children.

"Locals say that you should never leave your own children alone near the water or else La Llorona will take them to Heaven pretending that they are her own lost children.

"They say that they have heard her crying and wailing. They have heard her say, 'Ay, mis hijos' . . . 'Oh, my children'."

He paused in his narrative. His tone had been droning but then he broke from his script and leaned under the rooftop to ask,

"Why you want to go to Don Barerra's island so much?"

His voice was curious as he pushed the oar and slid the boat. Emily looked at her Mum. She was wearing sunglasses and looked out across the water without any movement at all. Paul looked at Emily.

"We're taking something back," he said and smiled at her.

Why the hell did he say that? Why say anything at all? Taking something back? What else would there be to take back except for a doll? The guide's eyes paused over each of them. He leaned over to look at the backpack that sat next to Emily's legs. He coughed lightly then resumed his rowing. He no longer spoke at all. The scripted narrative was abandoned. He pushed the gondola wordlessly leaving each of them to their own thoughts.

Her Mum remained statue silent. Paul seemed unperturbed by his own comments. He didn't seem to notice that the guide had stopped talking after he said what he said. Emily's brow was furrowed. He knows there's a doll in the bag. He knows we're taking it back. She knew that this meant something to him. Was this a silence of hatred or respect?

She looked at the guide. He effortlessly manoeuvred the boat between the islands. His face was without expression. She could not guess what he was thinking at all. Eventually she gave up and looked out at the islands they past. They were increasingly beautiful. Pink flowers bloomed and gave off a pungent, pleasant aroma that filled her with a sort of optimistic hope. Everything would be alright.

"La Isla de las Munecas," the guide said at last.

They approached wooden posts that lined the bank of an island. Above these were trees decorated with hanging dolls. They were tied to the trunks and branches of several trees. The sun had bleached their plastic faces to a ghostly white and some had cobwebs covering their features. Most of the dolls were fully intact but others were just a decapitated head or a severed limb.

The boat banged against the wooden posts and the guide tethered a rope around the longest one at the end.

"Follow the path to Don Barrera's home. I will wait here for you. If you don't want the full hour then that's fine. But don't be longer than one hour."

"We won't be," Catherine said as she alighted the boat.

Paul held out his hand for Emily to take it. She didn't and hopped onto the muddy bank. She had taken the back pack from him. It was over one shoulder and she peered into the trees. Paul thudded next to her.

"This way then," she said and led the way that she already knew.

It was the island from her dream. Everything was identical. The dolls in the trees were the same. She had made this journey before.

They walked along the path between the doll strewn trees. Emily fixed her eyes upon the ground. She had seen this all before and didn't particularly want to see it again. She had a job to do. Put the doll back into the shack and then leave. They'd be back at the hotel in no time. Paul and her Mum could sip cocktails and everything would be back to normal. They would have a week in Mexico to go sight-seeing, shopping and sunbathing.

They just had to do this first.

The bridge arrived in no time. The doll heads that lined each post didn't turn to her this time though. Thankfully. She dropped her shoulder and had the backpack in her hand now.

The shack was just beyond. Its doll covered walls glowed in the afternoon sun. She looked at her watch. It was not long after five.

She recalled the guide saying that they did night time tours. She couldn't imagine anything worse.

The inside was as she had seen before. Dolls on the wall and the floor. Dolls tied to the ceiling and window. Then there, right in the middle of the floor, among straw, was a pillow. An empty pillow. Kyle, what did you do? What were you thinking?

Emily unzipped the backpack and held out the doll.

"Casa," she heard herself say.

She placed the doll gently down upon the pillow. There was reverence and ceremony in her actions. Should she say something? The doll seemed smaller than before. It looked so innocent as it laid upon the soft pillow staring up at the ceiling. It looked at peace. It was done. They had taken her home.

She looked at Paul and her Mum.

"Right, let's go then."

Her Mum turned and walked out of the shack. Paul followed. Emily looked for one last time at the doll. She looked so serene. Happy even. It was all over. Now her life would be back to normal. Now she could get on with the things that made her happy. Shopping, friends . . . sleep even.

They walked swiftly between the trees and back to the muddy bank. A smile found its way upon her lips. She felt like some massive weight had been lifted from her shoulders. She felt as if the pressure of the last few days and nights were finally gone. The backpack was empty in her hand. It hadn't weighed much before but now felt utterly weightless, like she was carrying a helium filled balloon.

She darted past Paul and held her Mum's hand. Catherine looked at Emily. She smiled and it was returned.

"Wait," Paul said from behind, "What?"

They looked back at him. His face stared beyond them. They looked and saw what he saw.

The boat was gone.

"No," Paul said, pushing past them, "He can't have just left us."

He hurried down to the wooden posts at the edge of the water and looked in all directions.

"He has!" he said, almost hysterically, "He's left us!"

Emily did wonder why Paul had paid the guide before they had even left the harbour but decided it would be utterly pointless to bring this up.

"He might be just turning around," she said instead.

All three of them looked in every direction. There was bird song and the strong smell of flowers. The air was warm. They waited.

He didn't return. There was no sign of any boat at all. Another island was close. Perhaps they should swim over to that? At least it had no dolls on it.

Catherine sat down on the muddy bank. Paul looked at her, sighed and did the same.

"The guide said that there were night time tours," he said, "Someone will be back tonight."

Night time. That meant darkness. Alone on an island with dolls and darkness. Emily could think of nothing worse. She stood looking down at her Mum and Paul and saw white dots zoom over her vision. They raced and fizzed all around. She felt as if she wasn't really there. Dizziness overcame everything. She felt that if she didn't sit down then she would stumble and fall into the water yet she couldn't move.

She took in a deep breath and tried to close her eyes but found she couldn't. She continued to breathe deeply for a few moments and the white dots disappeared.

Paul was right. There would be a night time tour. They just had to wait until it was dark.

She took in one huge breath and then exhaled slowly through her nose. Sighing, she sat down next to them. Paul put his arm around her. His other arm was around her Mum.

She looked at them both and tried to ignore the dolls that hung above. They wore the masks of children and swayed in the trees impassively watching them. They would sit there below. Just sit there and wait. Wait for the boat that would come. Come and rescue them.

Emily looked at her watch again. Five thirty. Almost.

"What time does it get dark?" she asked.

Paul took out his phone.

"No signal," he said, "Check yours."

Emily turned her phone on. Her Mum wordlessly showed Paul her own phone.

"No signal either," he sighed.

Both Paul and her Mum looked at Emily and waited while the screen changed from the Apple symbol to an image of her, Ngozi and Meg.

The phone took its time and finally told them it had no signal either.

"So, what time does it get dark?"

The question remained unanswered and they sat and waited.

Chapter Thirty-Two

They waited for another three hours. It was eight thirty PM. All three of them took turns to alternately look from the winding canals to their phones. The minutes ticked away impossibly slowly. Time was drenched in a sticky solution that made it slither slowly around them.

The sky changed colour before their very eyes. It went from a vivid blue and white to a vast stretch of yellow then endless shades of orange. It was like a huge sheet above their heads was having droplets of coloured ink dripped upon it by some divine being in the sky. The colours spread quickly and changed constantly. The oranges gently became darker and more red. The sun glowed dimly and descended into the serpentine canals that snaked it away into its murky depths.

Darkness was coming.

They sat huddled together endlessly hoping to catch sight of a boat in the distance.

"He said there would be a night time tour."

Paul's voice was a rasping croak. None of them had spoken for some time and his voice was dry.

"A night time tour means that they must arrive when its dark. So, this is good. The dark is what we've been waiting for. It's good."

This was said as if it wasn't a question but it felt like it was. It felt as if he wanted their reassurance and affirmation.

There was now only a thin layer of orange above the water. Above this were bands of fading dark blue that battled against the ever-increasing darkness that descended in relentless waves. At last, the darkness won. It pounded the light from the sky and, in a cry of victory in battle, a rumble of thunder echoed in the distance.

The air instantly chilled as the light left them. Tendrils of ice slithered ever so gently over their exposed skin. Hairs on legs were raised, goosebumps were teased out and shivers ran down spines involuntarily.

Emily didn't want to look up but she did. The dolls were there. Of course they were, still hanging with eyes that bore down on onto her. Their faces seemed to glow white in the darkness making their black sockets even blacker against the ghostly pale of their pallid skin.

Emily's eyes darted away. How long would they be here? They had returned the doll. They had done what it wanted so why where they still on this island? They weren't longer than one hour yet the guide had left them. Had this been deliberate? Maybe he needed to get back to bring the night time tour along and them pick them up. But they'd been left here on their own for over three hours. She looked at her phone again. She had seven percent of her battery left.

Her Mum and Paul took out their phones too. The little rectangles of light were a source of distraction but brows creased as they saw their own battery life seemed to drain before their eyes.

A fork of lightning flashed in the sky. White light zipped across the darkness lighting up the sky and the island for a brief moment. Then thunder rumbled again. Closer this time.

They exchanged glances. The first inevitable droplets of rain then came. The sound of splashing rain thudded onto the water in front of them. It fell in large blobs heavily thwacking the surface of the canals. Then it fell onto the trees, the canal bank and onto them.

Catherine stood first then Emily and Paul stood either side. They huddled together and the rain began to pour even heavier. Lightning flashed across the sky again and the thunder followed close behind like some sinister and very audible shadow. It growled. It was a predator unlike any other as it proudly announced its approach angrily and loudly. Its prey was trapped and it was enjoying the hunt.

"We have to stay here," Paul said breathlessly, "We won't hear the boat from anywhere else."

But they all knew that if the storm increased then the canal boat would never make the journey. The boats simply weren't designed to travel through adverse weather conditions. Their design was made for sleek and smooth movement. To silently slide over calm waters. The water of Xochimilco now fizzed and bounced against the sides of the banks in ever increasingly larger waves.

To taunt then further, the lightning flashed and the thunder roared right above them. The rain was warm but they huddled and shivered in its heavy downpour. Then the wind began to join the assault. It grew stronger and pushed at them from all sides. It whipped up the rain and threw it down upon them. The lighting flashed and the storm increased its attack. They were just too exposed on the canal bank. It hammered at them all around. They squatted onto the floor still clutching at each other with eyes closed and faces screwed up tight. Even from behind closed lids they could see the flash of light from above. Soon it would pass over them, surely. They were certain of it. Longed for it. But it didn't. The rain and the wind worked as one to roar and lash down again and again.

"We need to get shelter!"

Paul's voice was like an echo is in the distance. Emily felt a firm grip of four hands pulling at her. Shelter? But where? In the shack of dolls? It was absurd. Yet she was being dragged toward it.

The storm pursued them into the woods and along to the bridge. The dolls were also being hammered by the rain but looked on nonchalantly as the trio staggered toward the hut. Some of the dolls tethered to ropes had come loose and were wildly flapping in the wind, banging against the trees in silent torture over and over again, flailing relentlessly.

They paused at the entrance to the shack. The roof rattled and the darkness within seemed immense. This was the only shelter on the island yet seemed like the worse place to be. Paul pulled Emily and her Mum inside. He slammed the door shut and they felt the rain and wind instantly subside.

They dripped noisily onto the straw strewn floor and looked around. The dolls seemed to glow here in the sparse light too. There was no glass in the window frame so the storm found its way inside but to a much lesser degree. It was the sound that had intensified however. The rain pounded onto the corrugated tin roof. The sound waves bounced back from ceiling to floor to ceiling again and again. It was like being inside a speaker with the volume up to one hundred. It filled the space utterly.

They crouched again and held on to one another. Speaking would be useless. There would be no way of being heard. Emily took out her phone from her sodden leggings. It was completely lifeless. She didn't know if the battery was dead or if it was soaked through. The screen and back were slippery with moisture. She slid it into her pocket.

She found her eyes wandering over to the doll she had brought to her home. The other dolls all sat attentively around while she was laid peacefully upon her makeshift bed. She stared contently upward seemingly enjoying the vast sound of the storm. Each raindrop sounded like a fist being hammered above like the fists of a million dolls.

Emily couldn't take her eyes of the doll. She fixed her gaze upon it and found herself willing the doll to make the storm stop. To make this all stop. But she was lifeless. She did nothing to help.

After an age had passed the wind died down and the rain became less heavy. The pounding above gave way to tapping. The howling wind became a soft whispering. The roof had a rhythmic dripping. Rivets of rain fell from between the grooves of the corrugated roof. They watched from the window and saw thin waterfalls descending in ordered lines.

They rose as one. Paul released his grip but Emily and her Mum still held on to one another. They stretched aching limbs and backs.

The storm rumbled on in the distance growing quieter as it retreated. They shivered and with grim resignation, Emily realised that although this was now better, no rescue party would arrive this night. Even though the storm had passed surely any night time tour was cancelled. They would be here until morning. What then, she didn't know.

"Should we go back to the bank?" Catherine asked.

Emily looked at her Mum. Desperate eyes went back and forth. Paul eventually shook his head.

"No one is coming tonight," he said at last as if confirming Emily's thought process. Their faces were ashen and pale in the gloom. They looked around at the dolls inside.

"Shall we take them out?" Paul asked, "Clear this place and try to get some sleep?"

Sleep? Emily almost burst out laughing but didn't. She looked at the dolls then back to Paul. Taking the dolls out seemed wrong. They had travelled half way around the world to return a doll to this very home and now he was talking about taking them out of this home and going to sleep. She shook her head in disbelief and he nodded back to her as if her incredulous gesture was an answer to his question.

Then there was a knock on the other side of the closed door.

Emily heard herself give a sharp intake of breath then held it. Her eyes were instantly wider and she looked at Paul and her Mum. They had heard it too. Their bodies stiffened and muscles were clenched everywhere.

Then it came again. Three gentle taps on the sodden wood. They were hollow and dull sounding. They came from low down on the door.

No one moved. The water no longer ran from the roof but the dripping continued. The horizontal wooden slats of the walls dripped too. If it wasn't for that sound it would have seemed that time had entirely stopped. They each were statues in the shack.

Eventually, Emily's eyes found the window. It was so exposed. Anything could get in.

Then the knocking came again. Three raps, more urgent now with less space in between.

They jumped as three more knocks came but this time from behind them. It was on the walls of the shack from the outside.

Then more knocking from the opposite side. From all sides. All in perfect timing as if following a score on a sheet of music. Knock, knock, knock, with a pause and repeat, but building in force each time.

Emily felt her mind being dissected piece by piece. Her sanity was being dismantled. This couldn't be happening. It was just not possible.

More knocking. Again and again. Louder each time. It was coming from the door, the walls, the roof; louder and louder. It made the shack shake and they quivered within. Their heaving chests were panting with fear and desperation. Their wild eyes everywhere. There was no *one* source to the sound. It was everywhere.

But then it came from within the shack. They whirled around to see what had made it. It came from the side. From behind. From in front. From the shadows. But there was no movement that they could see. Every time they turned, every time they looked, the knocking came from the other direction.

And still it got louder. Emily started screaming. She fell to the floor with her hands clamped over her head. She clutched her hair in tight clumps, her knuckles white and shaking. Her Mum fell upon her and then Paul.

The knocking was all over them, no longer in threes but just a constant hammering noise that was everywhere. It engulfed them. It devoured them in its immense volume. Their screams were drowned out by it. It shook the walls, the floor and them in an ocean of noise.

Emily screamed on until her throat burned and her lungs were empty. Then she passed out. Darkness engulfed her. She slipped out of consciousness and drifted into the deep and inky waters of nothingness.

Chapter Thirty-Three

THE FIRST SHAFTS OF light crept over the canals of Xochimilco in golden fingers. They stretched over the water and onto the islands. La Isla de las Munecas was illuminated in white light. The dolls were bathed in it. Their tiny features lit up one by one as the morning sun evaporated the water from the storm the night before.

The rays penetrated the leaf strewn floor between the trees and made its way to the shack of Don Julian. Crawling slowly onward.

Inside the shack were three new dolls. They were laid upon the floor, heaped on top of one another, forever silent and content beside their companions. They had pride of place. They would forever share the home of the drowned girl; Agustinata. It would be their honour to spend an eternity with her.